Romanced

by a

SEAL

HOT SEALS

Cat Johnson

ISBN-13: 978-1532719028
ISBN-10: 1532719027

CHAPTER ONE

Dusk had already fallen when Jon parked his truck in the lot.

The early spring air was overly warm for this time of year, but having been to almost every hellhole on the planet, he'd take a balmy evening in Virginia any day.

He pushed through the scarred wooden door, exchanging the evening shadows outside for the perpetually dim interior of the dive bar.

It was a good time and a good place for the meet, though it had taken a bit of fancy talking on his part to get away from Ali just before dinner.

Tomorrow while she was at work it would have been so much easier for him to get away, but as things came to a head, this meet with his contact couldn't wait.

When the man had sent the signal to set up the rendezvous, Jon had sucked it up and lied to his now live-in girlfriend. What the hell else could he do?

He hadn't known what he'd been about to get involved in when he and Ali had discussed her moving in with him a few months ago.

Hindsight always was twenty-twenty.

Tonight she'd come home after a full day at her job and had worked hard to cook him a beautiful homemade meal. One which he couldn't stick around long enough to eat.

He'd made a bullshit excuse about why he had to leave the house and he'd seen the resulting look in her eyes. Part anger. Part disappointment.

The look wasn't the worst of it. That had been delivered with a single blow. One word said in a tone so dismissive it was like a dull knife carving a hole in his gut.

"Fine."

What was it about that word—*fine*—that got to him? That single measured syllable seemed so much worse than if she'd yelled or cursed at him.

Hell, anything would have been better, because it was clear from the glare and her body language that things were not fine at all.

He didn't have time for this. Not now. Not given what he was involved in. His life was about to change radically and Ali couldn't be a part of any of it. He needed to remember that, pocket his emotions and forge ahead.

Spotting his contact in the back, half hidden in a dark corner lit only by a dusty neon beer sign. His face was in shadow beneath a baseball hat pulled low.

Jon made his way over.

The man watched him walk. No one else in the

bar noticed Jon's arrival or seemed to care. That's why they'd set this place for the meet. It always had a mix of drunks who couldn't give a shit what went on around them.

It was definitely not a place Jon would usually visit for fun . . . or unarmed, which is why he'd strapped on his leg holster.

That feeling of being naked without a weapon was his own issue to be worked on. A result of seeing and doing too much in his thirty-something years on Earth.

"Rudnick." Hasaan barely raised his eyes as he lifted his beer bottle and downed a swallow.

"Hasaan." Jon nodded as he scanned past the few patrons in the establishment. "There a waitress here?"

Hasaan snorted out a laugh. "What do you think?"

"Yeah. I figured. Another one?" he asked.

"Hell, yeah. Thanks." The man—probably about the same age as Jon—tipped his head as Jon turned toward the bar.

No surprise his contact was downing the beer. No one would want to be in this place sober, that's for sure.

In fact, Jon might have to leave his shoes outside the door of the condo when he got home. The way each step stuck to the floor, God only knew what was on it.

"Hey, how's it going?" The bartender looked like he doubled as a bouncer judging by the thickness of his neck and forearms, and the scar slicing across his upper lip.

"Good, thanks. Two longnecks, please."

"You got it." The bartender opened the bottles and planted them on the dinged bar top.

Jon threw a bill down and grabbed the two bottles. "Thanks. Keep the change."

The man nodded his gratitude and Jon headed back to the corner where they'd have privacy for their business. More than that, he'd avoid a conversation with the lone drunk seated on a barstool and talking back to the news anchor on the television hanging above the bar.

In Jon's experience, there were good dive bars and bad ones. Arnold's Tiki Bar, hidden away down the end of a narrow alleyway in Waikiki, with its three-dollar Longboards and five-dollar Mai Tais, was a good dive bar.

This shit hole—not so much. There was good reason he'd never been here and why he wouldn't have to worry about seeing anyone he knew.

That served him well for their purposes tonight.

He set the bottles down with a plunk and pulled out a chair, eyeing it to make sure there was nothing disgusting on the seat that he could carry home on his pants.

No one knew he was here tonight. No one knew what he was involved in. Not his business partner Zane, not his friends, and not his girlfriend Ali—and it needed to stay that way.

"Any problems?" his contact asked.

Keeping his eye trained on the door and the drunk at the bar, just in case, Jon said, "Nope. Did you expect any?"

"From you? No. Not really."

Jon chose to take that as a compliment.

After all of the years he'd spent training and working, Jon was well equipped for what he was currently involved in. But of course, one couldn't get complacent when it came to dealing with Daesh, aka ISIS, aka ISIL.

It didn't matter what name the press used for the group, the facts remained the same. As an organization, they were deadly and they were savvy. But now they were also on the defensive as they tried to hold on to the regions they'd taken control of so easily just a couple of years ago.

That could make them desperate and dangerous.

Like a fighter against the ropes, ISIS would fight even harder rather than go down. And Jon was going to help them.

"When was last contact?" Hasaan asked, keeping his voice low.

"Two days ago." The message had come through the mobile messaging app Jon had been using for the past months to connect with the ISIS recruiter.

Did the creators of the app realize that the end-to-end encryption provided the perfect venue for untraceable communications? Did they care?

"Is everything in place?" Hasaan asked, pulling him back to the conversation.

"Yes." Jon lied smoothly, as he always did.

Contact had been made. Plans set in motion. Exact dates and times would come next. That was all true, but as far as everything else being ready?

No. Not quite.

Lying to his partner Zane and the guys who worked for their company had been one of the most difficult things he'd ever had to do.

Hiding the truth from Ali had been even worse. He saw the anger in her every time he skirted a question or disappeared. The secrecy was driving a wedge between them, harming his relationship with her and with his teammates.

The overall cost of what he was doing could be high. The damage possibly irreversible.

The stress of it all was affecting him physically. Jon had to consciously unclench his jaw repeatedly throughout the day and when he woke in the middle of the night.

He had to believe it was worth it and forge ahead, no matter what the risk.

"You sure you're ready for this?"

The question had Jon pulling his attention from observing the room and looking directly at Hasaan. He found the man's full gaze leveled on him.

Drawing his brows down in a frown, Jon asked, "You doubting me?"

"No. You doubting yourself?"

"Of course not."

"What you're getting into is dangerous shit."

"I've been in dangerous situations before."

Seemingly satisfied with that answer, Hasaan tipped his head in a nod of acceptance, while Jon tried to quiet the voice in his head.

The danger he was about to walk into was different. This time there was no government backing him. No teammates to watch his six. No friend to break the news to Ali should anything happen—he squashed that thought before it fucked with his head any more than it already had.

Downing the remainder of the beer, Jon planted the bottle on the table and shot Hasaan a glance.

"Let's wrap this up. I gotta get home."

Ali might be pissed at him, but a sudden need to get back to her rode him hard.

Hasaan tipped his head again, pushing the chair back with a loud scrape. He led the way to the men's room.

Inside the filthy room, in front of the single urinal, he reached beneath his shirt and pulled out an envelope. Handing it to Jon, he said, "Passport and cash."

Jon shook his head. "I don't need money—"

"It's local currency. There are times that American dollars might call unwanted attention to you over there and it's better if you don't appear on any bank surveillance videos exchanging US money."

Jon should have thought of that himself. He had to get his head back in the game.

He extended his hand to take the envelope. "Good thinking."

"It's my job." Hasaan hesitated before meeting Jon's gaze. "If the shit hits the fan—"

"I'll deal with it."

Hasaan's deep scowl and exasperated huff silenced any further comments Jon might have made. "Stop playing the bad ass and let me finish."

Jon pressed his lips together and nodded.

"There's a name and number written in that envelope. Memorize it then destroy it."

Brows raised, Jon glanced from the envelope to Hasaan. He knew well the *Amn al-Dawla*, ISIS's state security, monitored communications. A foreign recruit would be watched even more closely.

Although if the shit did hit the fan and he became compromised, avoiding detection by counterintelligence would no longer matter.

“Got it?” the man asked when Jon didn’t comment.

“Got it.” Jon extended his hand and shook Hasaan’s. “Thanks.”

Maybe he wasn’t completely on his own in this thing after all.

CHAPTER TWO

Too angry to eat the dinner she'd spent hours shopping for and preparing, Ali yanked hard on the kitchen drawer.

Just like everything else in Jon's life, even the drawers in his condo were neatly organized. Rolls of plastic wrap lined up in precision formation amid aluminum foil and boxes of plastic bags in every size.

The sight only ramped up her anger.

Everything in Jon's existence was in perfect order *except* for his relationship with her.

She was the messy junk drawer of his life.

That realization had her pausing, hand on the plastic wrap. No wonder he avoided spending time at home with her. Running out at every opportunity. Each excuse plausible but seeming more flimsy than the last.

It had been a mistake moving in together. Just

because something made financial sense didn't mean it was right.

Things between them had started to go downhill shortly after she'd moved in so it was pretty obvious to her that this decision, though practical, had been very, very wrong.

Hot angry tears pricked behind her eyes as she grabbed the wrap and yanked to tear off a piece.

The clingy plastic got tangled on the sharp serrated edge. She pawed at it but only ended up cutting her finger instead of the clear wrap.

"Shit." Tossing the whole mess onto the counter, she shoved the stinging finger in her mouth and sucked at the thin stripe of red that appeared.

One handed as she nursed her wound, she grabbed her food-laden plate from the counter, intent on shoving it onto the fridge shelf uncovered.

Unwrapped food in the refrigerator—that would drive Jon crazy. Perfect. It would teach him for walking out—

again—this time after she'd gone to so much trouble to make a nice meal for him.

The spiteful thought had her feeling quite satisfied as she spun toward the fridge . . . and jumped as a scream tore from her throat.

That was followed directly by a huff of frustration. "Dammit, Jon. Will you please make some noise when you come in? You scared the hell out of me."

"Sorry." He tracked her with his eyes from where he stood in the kitchen doorway as she moved to the refrigerator.

Judging by the one brow he cocked up as he

watched her, he definitely took notice of the unwrapped dish she shoved inside.

She closed the door and leveled a gaze on him, silently daring him to say a word. That he didn't comment surprised her.

"What happened to your finger?" He lifted a chin toward the finger she held up in the air so she didn't get blood on her clothes.

"I cut it on the plastic wrap box."

He moved forward and took her hand in his, inspecting the wound. "You should clean it and put on a bandage."

"It's not that deep." She hated that she couldn't control how her heartbeat sped when he touched her.

"It could still get infected." Standing close, he didn't drop his hold on her hand.

She raised her gaze and found he was focused solely on her.

Those piercing blue eyes of his had gotten to her starting the first day she saw him on Rick and Darci's front doorstep. When he looked at her like this, the depth of the feelings hidden within Jon's eyes could still make her weak in the knees.

"Okay." She felt breathless as she only vaguely remembered what she was agreeing to.

She reminded herself how often lately she'd seen those eyes go hard and cold as Jon slammed the wall down between them.

Drawing in a shaky breath she pulled her hand from his grasp.

He let her, but it was only to reach out and pull her body close. Holding her tight against him with the hands he clamped on her hips, Jon dropped his head and took possession of her mouth with a demanding kiss.

She wanted to stay angry.

Wanted to pull away and punish him, not give him what he wanted, but it seemed so long since he'd touched her. And it felt so good to know he still wanted her. She'd begun to doubt that as he became more distant and obsessed with work.

At least she'd hoped it was work and not something or *someone* else. She'd begun to doubt that too.

But right now there was no doubt what he wanted as he plunged his tongue against hers while backing her against the cabinets.

His grip tightened around her middle as he lifted and set her up on the counter to the side of the sink.

The space was clear since nothing was ever left out or out of place in this household.

His neat streak would make having sex on the kitchen counter easy. Not that they'd ever done that . . .

He shoved the hem of her skirt up to her thighs before reaching higher and yanking her underwear all the way down her legs.

"Jon, what are you doing?" Her eyes flew wide. "Here?"

Not answering, he stepped closer and leaned low between her thighs. When his tongue connected with her core she didn't need him to answer.

"We can go to the bedroom . . . " Her suggestion trailed off as he pushed two fingers inside, attacking her on two fronts and making her forget that she had complained about their location.

She sucked in a breath at the sensations shooting through her. He always had known exactly how to touch her.

Sex—when he had the time and the inclination to have it—had always been good between them.

More than good. Great. No matter how they'd drifted apart she couldn't deny that.

Certainly not now as the heat of his mouth and the motion of his touch pushed her closer to the edge.

Seconds later she plunged into an orgasm that had her eyes slamming shut and her head thrown back. She gripped the edge of the countertop, feeling the need to hang on to something solid as her body spiraled out of control.

Her muscles still pulsed when he pulled back. Deft hands left her to unbuckle his belt and then open his pants.

Jon lifted her off her perch and lowered her onto his cock.

She hated every hour he spent lifting weights in the makeshift gym he'd created in the back room of the GAPS office, but she had to admit the workouts had visible results. Through the sheer strength of his arms, he braced against the cabinets as he plunged inside her over and over.

His breath came fast and loud from the exertion as he sped his motion. He came with a loud groan, his body shuddering to completion inside her.

Seconds ticked by—him still inside her, her still held up by his strength—before he set her feet on the floor.

Still breathing heavily, he quickly fixed his pants and then rested his forehead against hers. "I'm sorry I missed dinner."

Did he expect her to say that it was all right?

That wasn't going to happen. Not this time.

She drew in a breath and kept her lips firmly shut, until she couldn't keep quiet any longer. "This—what we just did—doesn't mean anything. I'm still mad at you."

He bent to scoop up her underwear from the floor. Handing them to her he nodded. "I know you're still mad, but this couldn't wait."

Sex couldn't wait?

Why not? Where was he going? What was he doing and for how long? She almost asked, and then thought better of it.

Why bother asking? Chances were he wouldn't tell her anyway and it hurt worse when he dodged the question than if she just didn't ask at all.

"Come to bed?" His eyes narrowed with need as he brushed his thumb along her jawline.

Whether this sudden attention was to make up for lost time or to store up for when he was away—yet again—on some undisclosed danger-filled job, she didn't know. But apparently Jon wasn't done yet.

As much as she wanted to say no, his wanting her was too much for her to resist. It always had been that way between them.

Ali swallowed away the dryness in her throat. "Okay."

They could fight about everything that was wrong between them tomorrow.

Tonight she was smart enough to take advantage of having the version of Jon she'd fallen in love with back . . . before he disappeared again.

CHAPTER THREE

The sound of the cell vibrating on the nightstand knocked Jon out of sleep. He reached for it, gripping it tight in his fist to control the noise. Even on vibrate it seemed incredibly loud in the quiet of the bedroom lit by only the pale light of pre-dawn.

He strode across the room and out the door, pulling it closed behind him before he answered. "Rudnick."

"You were still sleeping?" Zane sounded surprised.

Jon drew in a deep breath and glanced at the closed bedroom door.

Hopefully Ali had slept through the phone call.

They'd declared a truce last night—twice—but he knew the fight would resume as soon as she woke and he'd at least like to have some coffee in his system before it did.

"I was up late. What's up?" It had to be

something for Zane to be calling this early.

Of course, perhaps he had a six a.m. tee time with the senator or something. Now that Zane was spending more of his time in the Capital than here, thanks to Senator Greenwood's daughter Missy, anything was possible.

"You see the news?"

Jon ran his hand over his face and drew in a bracing breath. "No. What happened?"

"A SEAL was killed in northern Iraq."

"Fuck. ISIS?" Jon guessed.

"Yes. Reports are pretty sketchy this early. One said a couple of hundred fighters broke through the line at a checkpoint and hit a village. He was sent in as part of a quick reaction force."

"They release a name yet?" Jon asked.

He'd been keeping his voice down to not wake Ali, but still he glanced again at the bedroom door as he moved toward the kitchen.

"Not yet." Zane's tone was grave.

No doubt they were both thinking the same thing. There was a good chance they'd know the man who'd been killed since he and Zane had only recently left the teams.

Hell, half of their friends were still active duty.

Jon started an inventory in his brain to try and remember if his old team was currently stateside or away. He'd have to text Chris Cassidy and see if his brother Brody was home or away. That would give him the answer.

God, he hoped the team wasn't in Iraq. One of Brody's teammates, Rocky, had just gotten married. His new wife Izzy would be going crazy if she saw this on the news while Rocky was away.

Fuck. This shit needed to end. Not in a decade. Now.

More determined than ever to go through with his plan, Jon reached for the bag of coffee.

"I'm going to set up a meeting for as soon as I can." Zane's voice brought Jon back to the conversation.

"A meeting regarding what?" Jon asked.

"If that operator was really there as part of an *advise and assist* mission like they're reporting, I'm thinking the powers that be might be open to a proposal from a private contractor to come in and work in that capacity. Less bad press for the government if one of us is killed helping the Peshmerga than one of their golden boys."

Jon let out a snort. "We were their golden boys once."

"Which is why GAPS is the perfect choice for them to hire." There was a smile in Zane's tone.

Competitive to the bone. Zane always did have the end goal uppermost in his mind.

In this case that goal was a contract that would send GAPS to Iraq to train the Kurdish and Iraqi troops in how to defeat ISIS, all while trying to maintain the tenuous alliance between the two.

But Zane was right. GAPS would be perfect for the job. "All right. See what you can do."

"You'll drive up to make the presentation with me?"

Jon hesitated. "I'll try."

There was a pause on Zane's end as well. "What else do you have going on?"

And here comes the lie. "Just a couple of things going on here I might have to be around for."

"Give it to one of the other guys. This is important."

"We'll see. Set the meeting first then we'll worry about timing."

As long as Jon was up in the air waiting for his contact to give him his traveling orders, lying had been even more difficult than it would normally be.

He hated not having all the information. By the look of how things were going, he would have to get used to operating in the dark.

He hated deceiving his best friends and the woman he loved. He'd always had to keep details confidential while he was in the teams, but this was different.

This deception went far deeper. But again, lying to everyone he cared about was something he was going to have to get over.

Zane let out an audible sigh. "All right. But if you can make it, that would be great."

"I hear you. I'll do my best."

"Okay. Talk to you later." The silence on the other end of the line as Zane disconnected told Jon he didn't have to bother saying goodbye.

He shoved his cell in his pocket and was happy to have two hands to use to get the coffee going.

If Zane was annoyed now over Jon possibly missing a meeting, what was he going to do when Jon disappeared completely?

Yeah, that would go over like a lead balloon.

He'd need to repair a few damaged relationships after this was over. Ali. Zane. Probably Rick and

Chris would be pissed too.

God only knew who else would be angry when he left without explanation and then went completely dark. No communications with anyone for at least three months and that was *if* everything went as planned.

Jon blew out a breath.

It had to be done. This latest casualty proved that. No amount of advisors, no matter how highly trained, was going to eradicate a threat as deeply entrenched as ISIS was.

The battle would go on for years resulting in thousands more casualties on both sides, both military and the civilians caught in the middle. ISIS fighters, and the Iraqi, Kurdish and Syrian troops—they were all canon fodder at this point.

Defeating this enemy required precision.

A surgical cutting out of the cancer that had taken hold and spread, and Jon intended to be the man wielding the scalpel.

The coffee had just started to stream into the carafe when the bedroom door opened.

"Morning. Coffee's on." He braced himself for the rampage.

"Okay. Thanks." Ali shuffled in her slippers and overly long pajama pants and leaned into him.

Surprised, but happy, he wrapped his arms around her. "Tired?"

"Yeah. Somebody kept me up late."

"Sorry." He smiled, not feeling bad at all.

"Who called so early?"

"Zane."

She groaned against his chest at hearing his

partner's name.

Jon laughed at her reaction. In spite of Zane's infamous reputation with the ladies, Ali had never fallen under his spell. Lucky for Jon or he might not have ever had a shot with her.

She pulled away and looked up. "Will you be around tonight?"

He wished he could give her a yes or no but the truth was he didn't know.

If a message came, he could be gone on a moment's notice. He screwed up his mouth and considered how to answer. "Ali, I don't—"

She held up a hand to stop him. "Don't worry. I'm not cooking a big dinner. I learned my lesson. I'm not doing that again."

He figured he deserved that so he stayed quiet and let her continue.

"Darci invited everyone over. I'll go if you're around or not, I just wanted you to know." She might have woken up sweet and snuggly this morning, but the chill from his missing dinner last night lingered just beneath the surface.

"If I don't have a meeting, I'll be there. Promise."

"Okay." Turning away from him, but not before he saw her scowl, she reached for the coffee pot. "Can you grab two mugs?"

"Sure."

Things were sounding back to normal, but not really. He was smarter than to believe that.

He had to remember his end goal, which brought up the next question. "Did Darci say who will be there? Is Brody home?"

Ali shook her head. “No. She said as far as Chris knows the whole team is away. He didn’t know where or for how long—as usual.”

Her statement was accompanied by the usual annoyance visible in her expression. Ali was the type of person who wasn’t happy unless she knew all the facts. The exact opposite of the kind of woman who should have ever considered dating a SEAL, or even a former SEAL who still worked confidential jobs.

Yet here they were. Together.

He took the mug she’d filled for him. “I need to send a quick email.”

“Sure. Go ahead.” The weary tone in her voice belied the casual reply but he couldn’t let it get to him. Not now.

Sitting at his desk, he signed into his email account and sent a group message to Brody, Thom, Rocky, Mack and Grant. Then he typed one single line.

Check in!

After hitting send, he closed the browser and leaned back in his chair. Now, all he could do was wait—and worry—until one of the active duty guys replied or the media released the name of the SEAL who’d been killed.

No wonder Ali was so pissed off all the time. Being on this side of the action—the helpless, clueless, waiting side—sucked.

But the feelings inside him only fueled his determination to help end this bullshit.

He’d be in the action soon enough.

CHAPTER FOUR

Ali had braced herself all day for the inevitable—Jon backing out of going out tonight—which is why when he strode into the bedroom just as she was finishing getting ready to leave for Darci's, she had to do a double take.

"You're home."

He leaned against the dresser and nodded. "I am. You look nice."

Scowling, she glanced down at the outfit she'd put on. The waistband on the navy slacks was tight. So much so she'd had to put on a long loose blouse worn untucked to cover the straining buttons and zipper of the pants.

"Thanks." She was going to blame her recent weight gain on stress. That was her story and she was sticking to it.

With a sigh, she reached for the necklace on the dresser. It was a tiny silver heart Jon had bought her for Valentines Day. She loved it. She loved him.

What she didn't love was that he'd been so busy with GAPS business that was all he'd done for Valentines Day—hand the gift to her with a store bought card and then leave.

Maybe she was being a bitch but she'd have gladly traded this or any gift for time with him, for his undivided attention, just for a little while. But those things were in short supply in Jon's life.

She drew in and blew out a loud breath annoyed she couldn't get the clasp open.

"Let me." He pushed off the dresser and stepped behind her. Taking the necklace from her hands, he fastened it easily around her neck before leaning low. He brushed his lips against the side of her throat and groaned. "When do we have to leave?"

"Now."

"Hmm. Too bad." He took a step back and she got a look at his needy expression.

She turned to face him. "What's gotten into you lately?"

He frowned. "What do you mean?"

"You're more . . . amorous than usual."

He drew his brows lower. "That's not true."

"Okay. Fine." It didn't matter what he said, she knew what she knew.

Since she'd moved in there had been whole weeks when Jon hadn't laid his hands on her even once. Hadn't paid attention to anything except for his phone and his computer.

Jon shook his head, looking as if he was going to argue the point when Ali's cell phone rang. Darci's name and photo appeared on the display.

Happy for a distraction from an argument she didn't have the time or energy for, Ali reached for the cell and glanced up at Jon.

"It's Darci. She might need us to pick up something." Ali hit the button to answer the call. "Hey, Darci."

"Oh my God. You won't believe this." Her friend was crying, or maybe laughing. Possibly both at the same time.

It made it so Ali could barely understand her. "Darci, what's happening? What's wrong?"

"Chris just proposed."

Ali's mouth fell open. She was speechless for a beat before she lifted her eyes to meet Jon's gaze. Brow raised, he was obviously waiting to hear the answer to her question. When she'd recovered her power of speech Ali repeated, "Chris just proposed?"

Jon's eyes widened. He must be as surprised as she was. Chris and Darci had started dating a long while after she and Jon had. Chris and Darci weren't even officially living together yet.

Darci continued, "You know how Chris just drove home to Alabama with Brody? It was the weekend all that stuff happened with Rocky and Izzy."

"Yes."

"He went to ask his grandmother for her wedding ring so he could propose to me."

Ali drew in a breath. "Wow. That's great. I'm, uh, really happy for you."

It was horrible to feel envious of her best friend but Ali did. Jealousy. Envy. Anger, that it wasn't her wearing Jon's ring on her finger.

"You have to get over here right away so we can celebrate."

So tonight's get together had become an engagement party. "We were just about to leave."

"Good. Hurry up."

"Okay. See you soon." She disconnected the call, realizing now they'd have to stop and pick up a bottle of champagne or something as an engagement gift, which would delay their arrival.

That might be for the best. She needed to wrap her head around this news before facing Darci and that ring on her finger.

Cell phone still in her hand, she raised her gaze to Jon. "Chris asked Darci to marry him."

"Yeah, so you said." He narrowed his eyes. "You don't look very happy about it. I thought you liked Chris."

"I do."

Jon shook his head. "Then what's wrong?"

"Nothing. I guess I didn't realize they were at this point. They haven't been together for very long." She let out a bitter laugh. "Certainly not as long as we have."

He pressed his lips together in a thin hard line. "Ali—"

She held up her hand to stop him. "It was just an observation, Jon. I'm not asking you to make the ultimate sacrifice."

They'd already had this discussion, very recently too. Outside on Darci and Rick's deck right after Jon's SEAL friend Rocky had asked a woman he barely knew to marry him.

Ali didn't need to repeat that fight. All it would do is reinforce the reality that though Jon was fine with dating her, having sex with her, even living with her, he didn't feel the need to make it official and marry her.

He'd never used those exact words but that was the gist of their discussions.

He could claim it was the distraction of his business, or his constant travel, or whatever that kept him from being able to seal the deal and make their relationship legal, but that didn't change anything. The fact remained he didn't need or want them to be married.

No amount of excuses would ease the pain of that knowledge for Ali. It felt like a rejection, even when he held her as he said it.

Jon let out a breath and stepped forward. "I love you."

"I know." The tightness in her chest pressed on her heart and she couldn't bring herself to say *I love you* back.

"It's not a good time right now," he continued.

Not a good time. She'd heard that excuse from him before when they talked about marriage. The worst part about his argument was that it was so damn vague she couldn't even argue.

She stifled a laugh. "I know that too."

He brushed a thumb over her cheek. "We'll get there one day. I promise."

God how much she wanted to believe that promise. Believe in him. As Jon pulled her tight against his strong warm chest Ali fought back tears and wished she could believe him.

CHAPTER FIVE

The car ride was silent.

Usually Jon didn't mind a peaceful silence but the emotions radiating off Ali seemed incredibly loud. He could only be thankful they weren't driving too far.

He was more than happy when they finally arrived at Darci's place.

Chris opened the door, a wide grin on his face. "Hey."

Champagne bottle in one hand, Jon extended the other. "So, I hear congratulations are in order."

"You hear right." Chris shook Jon's hand and then accepted a hug from Ali. "Hey, darlin'. Darci's in the kitchen. You better go look at her ring. She's been dying to show it off to somebody and you're the first ones here."

Ali laughed. "Okay."

Jon couldn't help but be a little pissed that Chris

got a big genuine smile and even a laugh, when all Jon had gotten from Ali lately had been scowls.

Once they were inside the house and the women were huddled over the ring Jon asked, "You hear from your brother?"

"No." Chris pressed his lips into a tight line and shook his head.

He'd no doubt heard the news about the SEAL casualty too and was worried.

Jon understood how worried Chris must be about his brother. Hell, Jon was concerned about Brody and the team as well. Still, Jon had to comment on Chris's piss poor timing in the romance department.

"I gotta say, bud, this was one hell of a shit time for you to get engaged. You had to propose to her *tonight*? Just weeks after Rocky got married?"

One more of his friends getting hitched was the one thing Jon didn't need right now.

Not while he and Ali were already on the outs regarding that very topic. And not while he was preparing to leave the country for the most dangerous thing he'd ever willingly entered into.

Chris lifted his brows. "For one thing, I had my reasons. For another, I'm not getting any younger. None of us are. If you ask me, I waited too long."

"So, what? Your biological clock is ticking?" Jon asked with a snort.

"Isn't yours?" Chris cocked his head.

Jon blew out a loud breath. "No, not at all. The conversation about babies is not even on the table. Ali and I have got enough other things to fight about at the moment."

Chris's gaze settled on something just behind

Jon and he realized Ali and Darci were not all that far away and he hadn't kept his voice down.

If she had heard his comments, he'd definitely be hearing about it later.

Jon ran a hand over his face, but refused to turn around. He didn't need to see her face to feel the daggers she was shooting at his back.

Time to change the subject. "Anyway, I emailed Brody and some of the guys on the team but I haven't gotten a reply."

"I doubt you will. I haven't heard from baby brother since he left. Wherever he is, communications are at a minimum."

"Are you worried?"

"Yeah. Of course, but uncertainty is a constant state in the life we chose. You know that. Since I haven't heard from Momma and Daddy, and they'd be the first ones notified, I have to think that no news is good news. The media will release the name soon enough, then we'll know for sure. Until then, I'm keeping things business as usual."

How Chris could be so Zen, Jon didn't know. Hearing of yet another casualty made him want to grab a weapon, board a transport and make someone pay for that life.

In the teams he'd had to wait for orders to do anything. That had been one reason why he'd left the Navy and formed his own company. Yet now he was in the same *sit around and wait* mode as in the teams.

Military or civilian, it seemed waiting was a way of life.

Maybe Jon needed to take a page out of Chris's

book since he seemed to have this waiting game down to a science.

"You want a drink?" Chris asked.

Jon let out a loud breath. "God, yes."

Chris laughed at the enthusiastic response. "Then you've come to the right place. I highly recommend marrying into a family with Hollywood connections. My future brother-in-law's girlfriend sent over a case of thirty year old scotch as an engagement gift."

Jon's eyes widened. Rick's actress girlfriend Sierra Cox had sent a case of scotch? He had a feeling their old teammate had a hand in that choice of gifts.

"Well, damn. Does Rick have any other sisters besides Darci that I could date?" Jon laughed.

Chris leveled a gaze on him. "I'd keep my voice down if I were you. I reckon you're in enough trouble with Ali already."

"Yup. You're probably right." But the scotch would help.

Chris shook his head. "You know. You and Ali, you're just about the most perfect couple I've ever seen."

Jon drew back at that comment. "Are we?"

It certainly didn't feel like that.

"Yeah. You are. Trouble is, you're too dense to see it."

Jon let out a snort. "Thanks."

"That's what friends are for." Chris reached for a bottle. "Ice or straight up?"

He shot Chris a glare. "Ice in thirty year old scotch? Please, don't insult me. Straight up is perfect."

"Good choice." Chris nodded and splashed a good amount into a glass but then stopped. "Ali driving home?"

Jon glanced over and saw a champagne glass in her hand. "I wouldn't count on it."

"Then that's all you get. I guess you'd better drink up now so you can sober up later." Chris handed him the glass.

"I guess so." Suddenly Jon missed the good old days. Back when he and all the guys could drink all they wanted and then crash on Rick's sofa. No girlfriends. No worries. The memory brought up a good question. "Where is Rick anyway?"

"On his way with Sierra. And Darci invited Isabel over since she's on base all alone while Rocky's away."

The women would outnumber the men at this party, which was the opposite of how it usually was. There had been times in the past when this room had been packed full with SEALs, shoulder to shoulder in a circle, glasses raised.

With those who were still active away—and hopefully safe and sound—the male population had thinned considerably.

That thought brought up the other person who was missing.

"You contact Zane?" Jon asked.

Chris shook his head. "Didn't even think of it. You can call him if you want. Is he in D.C. hanging with his girl's daddy the senator?"

Jon bobbed his head. "Yeah, but he's also there trying to wrangle a meeting and a contract for

GAPS. He has his eye on Iraq."

Laughing, Chris nodded. "That sounds about right. Too bad the senator didn't get the nomination to be the GOP presidential candidate. Imagine what miracles Zane could pull off with POTUS as his father-in-law."

Jon snorted. "No kidding."

God, he hoped this gamble he was taking paid off.

It could just as easily ruin all of their reputations and destroy all they'd built with GAPS. It could also get him thrown in jail as a terror suspect, if not killed.

No wonder he couldn't sleep at night.

Jon took another sip of the whisky and relished the warmth as it burned through his body.

Maybe this was what he needed to put him to sleep at night. Sex hadn't done it last night. Hopefully the scotch would help put him out tonight.

CHAPTER SIX

"I really am happy for you."

"I might believe that if you didn't look quite so miserable." Darci cocked up one blonde brow.

"It's not you and Chris. Really. It's me. And Jon."

Darci laughed. "Seriously? You're using the *it's not you, it's me* excuse?"

Ali rolled her eyes. "You know what I mean."

"I know." Darci pursed her lips together. "At least Jon got out of the military. His quitting the teams should have helped things. No more secret missions and all that shit."

"You'd think that, but no. Now he's just as secretive with his GAPS stuff as he was when he was in the teams. If not more so. At least when he was in the Navy he didn't bring work home."

"Chris's assignments for GAPS seem pretty straightforward. I mean one time he wouldn't tell me exactly where he was going, only that it was overseas, but that's normal. He couldn't say. It was a government contract."

Compared to what Jon usually told Ali, which was next to nil, Chris had spilled quite a bit of detail.

"Well, you're lucky. Jon hides away in his office on the computer with the door shut. Of course, maybe he's not working at all. Maybe he's cheating on me."

"What?" Darci drew back, shaking her head. "No. I don't believe it."

"So, it's easier to believe he'd rather work and never spend time with me?"

"First of all, Jon owns the company. Chris just takes a job here and there. Big difference in workload and responsibility. Second, SEALs live and breathe secrecy. You know that."

"But as you said, Jon left the Navy."

"Yes, but he didn't leave the mindset. And he always did throw himself head on into his job. He's a workaholic. He lives to work, while Chris worked to make a living. They're different." Darci shrugged.

It sounded so logical when her friend laid it out in simple terms like that. It didn't feel logical living it.

"I guess I just thought after I moved in with him we'd get engaged. Hell, I thought *before* I moved in with him we would."

Darci drew in a breath. "I know and I'm sorry."

Ali felt bad for making Darci uncomfortable at a time she should be completely, over the moon happy. “You don’t have to be sorry. And please don’t feel bad that Chris proposed and Jon didn’t. I’m fine.”

“I do feel bad. It’s the one thing that makes today not perfect for me.”

“Now I’m *really* sorry.”

“No. I didn’t say that to make you feel bad. I want you to know I understand. But please remember, Chris is way older than Jon.”

“Not way older. Ten years, at most.”

“Ten years is a lot. If we don’t have kids until Chris is let’s say forty-five, then he’ll be sixty-three by high school graduation.”

Darci’s math equations weren’t going to work on Ali. She couldn’t envision Chris worrying about his age in relation to babies.

Worrying about how old the kid would have to be for him to teach him to shoot a gun—yes, Ali could definitely picture Chris doing that, but not whining about how old he’d be at the kid’s high school graduation.

This was all just Darci trying to smooth over the fact that Chris had proposed when Jon hadn’t.

“You’re just trying to make me feel better, aren’t you?”

“Maybe. Did it work?” Darci lifted a brow.

“Maybe.” Ali couldn’t be mad at her friend just because she picked a man who wasn’t afraid to commit. Tired of letting Jon ruin her mood, Ali vowed to have fun tonight. “Enough talking about me. Let’s celebrate. I love both of you guys. Hell, after this glass of champagne I even love Rick, even though I know your brother annoys you sometimes."

Darci eyed the bubbles in her glass. "I love how Rick's girlfriend sent over this case of very fine champagne for us along with the case of scotch for Chris."

Ali raised her glass. "That certainly doesn't hurt."

"No, it sure didn't." Darci laughed. "Rick and Sierra should be here in a couple of hours. The jetsetters are flying in from Miami."

"Convenient for us that Sierra's gifts arrived before she did."

"Of course, they did. Stars don't carry their own stuff. One phone call from her and the owner of the local liquor store was in his car and on the way over. Apparently, it's good to be famous."

"I guess so." Even as she agreed with her friend, Ali knew she didn't need an Academy Award like Rick's girlfriend Sierra to be happy.

All she wanted was Jon. All of him, not just the small pieces he was willing to give her. Ali took another sip and vowed to forget her own woes. Tonight she was here to celebrate with Darci and Chris.

Good thing there was plenty of champagne.

~ * ~

As the evening progressed, the gathering grew.

A couple of Darci and Ali's coworkers from the bank showed up.

Rick and Sierra breezed into the house with all of the fanfare one would expect from a star. Sierra with a burst of perfume and designer casual clothing. Rick with a complaint about the security lines at the Miami airport.

Rocky's wife Isabel even came, with her baby Lola.

Ali enjoyed talking to Izzy and holding the baby.

Even with all of the envy she felt, Ali couldn't begrudge Izzy for wearing Rocky's wedding ring. Not when the poor girl hadn't heard from her SEAL husband since he'd left on his last assignment. Ali knew exactly how that felt.

At least Jon was currently in the country and safe. That she could be grateful for. She concentrated on that and the other good things in her life. Good friends. Good food. Really good champagne.

In fact, Ali's plan to enjoy the party actually worked.

Her good mood lasted through quite a few of the bottles of bubbly.

Lasted all the way until the drive home when she turned to Jon. "Do you know anything about where Rocky is?"

He glanced at her from behind the wheel, looking more interested in her question than he had about anything else she'd said recently. "No. Why do you ask?"

"Izzy hasn't heard from him since he left. I thought you might know something—anything—that could put her mind at ease."

He shook his head. "I don't. Sorry."

She scoffed, not quite believing him.

"What?" he asked.

"I was just wondering if you'd tell me even if you did know something."

"Ali, you know how the military works."

"Yup." She also knew he liked to keep pointing that out even though he was out of the military now.

Jon continued, "In Izzy's case, I have to think no news is good news."

"Because they'll notify next of kin first for that SEAL they haven't released the name of yet?"

"You know about that?"

"Yup. Izzy told us. She's been glued to the news twenty-four/seven."

"She shouldn't watch."

"I know. That's what Darci and I both told her. It's hard. Unlike me, she's still new at this." Ali was an old hat at being kept in the dark.

She glanced to see if the shot had hit home. Jon drew in a breath but didn't say anything. It wasn't easy to get him riled up, which could be very annoying.

Ali was in the mood for a fight. That wasn't a bad thing. Sometimes it could be cathartic for a couple to have a knock down, drag out argument. Get everything out in the open and then make up.

Unfortunately, Jon would avoid conflict like the plague. All that did was motivate Ali to push him more.

Maybe they really weren't compatible.

The startling revelation hit her just as he reached out and squeezed her hand.

"Chris hasn't heard from Brody either. It's my guess the team is fine. They just can't get any communications out. I know from experience that sometimes getting the sat-comm set up is the hardest part of the mission." He glanced at her.

"Would it help if I texted Izzy and told her that?"

"Yeah, I think it might."

Jon tipped his head. "I'll do it as soon as we get home."

Home.

His home was her home now too. That was true with or without a marriage license or a wedding band on her hand. Maybe that was all that mattered.

It was times like this, when he was sweet and logical, that she felt guilty for thinking what they had wasn't enough.

Ali turned her head to study his profile as he focused on the dark road ahead. "I love you, you know. Even when I don't say it."

She'd been stingy with the words today when he'd said it to her and she'd refused to say it back. Seeing Izzy so worried, unable to talk to Rocky even if she wanted to, reminded Ali that she needed to put petty feelings aside.

A person never knew which words would be their last.

"I know." He gave her fingers a squeeze. "And I love you, even when I'm working."

She couldn't help the slightly bitter laugh that escaped her. "That's good because you're always working."

He had to pull his hand away from hers to swing the car into their driveway. Cutting the engine, he turned in the seat to look at her. "I'm not working tonight."

There was heat in his gaze.

This Jon made her knees weak. This man she'd take with or without a commitment or a ring. But over the past few months this version didn't show up nearly as often as he used to. Pretty much since he'd taken to growing that long beard.

As crazy as it sounded, it was almost as if the two things were tied together. Jon's beard. Jon's elusiveness.

But her old Jon was here now beneath the facial hair.

"I guess we should go inside and take advantage of that," Ali said.

His eyes narrowed. "Good idea."

CHAPTER SEVEN

"News."

"Go ahead." Jon scrubbed his hand over his face and tried to wake up enough to talk to Zane coherently.

Judging by the oddly early hours of his partner's last two calls, Zane's friend was adhering to an early to bed, early to rise work ethic.

That was pretty much the opposite of how the man used to operate in the old days. The days when he was single, living it up, and out every night with a different woman.

Given the evidence, Jon had to credit Zane's relationship with Missy for this change. Jon just wished Zane's new diligent work ethic didn't have to begin at dawn.

"They released the name. He was a west coast guy."

That meant it wasn't one of the guys from his

former team. Jon let out a breath of relief and then felt immediately bad. Some family had gotten a knock on the door that had changed their lives forever.

Still he couldn't fight the feeling of gratitude that this time it wasn't one of their friends.

"There's more," Zane continued in a tone that led Jon to think what he had to say wouldn't be good.

"All right."

"The meeting is a no go."

Jon frowned. With all of his connections, Zane usually got any meeting he wanted. "Why?"

"Because anyone looking to go in as advisors are pretty much persona non grata with the military right now. And we can thank whatever idiot planned a meet-up with the Kurds in a village five miles from ISIS-held territory."

Christ, Jon really needed to remember to grab some coffee before he picked up the phone with Zane. The man was too awake for Jon to deal with this early.

Projecting himself into motion, Jon worked his way to the kitchen to remedy the coffee situation. "You're going to have to explain that a little bit more to me."

"That SEAL had been sent in as part of a QRF to extract a group of combat advisors there to advise and assist. The advisors had gotten pinned down in the village by a hundred and fifty or so fighters and needed rescuing."

"Ah. Yeah. I can see how command won't want to hear from any more advisors at the moment.

They're not going to send anyone over while this is breaking in the press, even if we would have been smart enough to choose a location a little less hot for the meet."

"It's not just the shit choice of location. It seems like it was one fuck up after another. Those fighters knew exactly where to find that meeting and when, so obviously somebody didn't keep quiet. On top of that, ISIS put together a sizeable fighting force and broke through the line with twenty-vehicles and a damn bulldozer so somebody was asleep on the job. Who doesn't notice that kind of offense being assembled? Somebody fucked up."

"Agreed." Jon sighed. "So this lead is a dead end, but that's okay. We have more than enough work to keep GAPS busy."

Too much, actually, since Jon was very possibly not going to be around.

"Fuck that. I'm not giving up. I still think there's an opportunity here. If I can just get a meeting, we can present to them everything that their current contractor did wrong and how we would have handled it differently."

It was very easy to play Monday morning quarterback and review everything that went wrong after the fact. That was very different than being able to avoid the tragedy to begin with. He wasn't about to say that though.

Jon was already spread too thin. He needed to choose his battles. With Zane. With Ali. And if Zane was off chasing meetings and out of Jon's hair, even better.

With that in mind, Jon said, "Okay. Keep

trying."

"Will do. I'll keep you informed."

"Great. Thanks." Jon was about to say goodbye and hang up when he remembered the latest news. "Oh and by the way, Chris asked Darci to marry him."

"Jesus. Is he trying to kill us all?"

Jon knew why he couldn't even think about proposing to Ali right now, but he was interested in Zane's reasons for being so adamant about not marrying Missy. "So, no ring for you and Missy? I figured you two would have been next. Why haven't you proposed yet?"

Zane snorted. "Because my father wants me to."

Jon laughed. Zane always had done the opposite of what his father wanted. It was what made him join the SEALs. "Understood. How does she feel about it though?"

"She's cool with it. Her name being my new tattoo helped."

"Your new tattoo?" Jon had to think that a tattoo was more of a commitment than a wedding ring, so it probably did make Missy happy. He couldn't copy Zane now. Too bad he hadn't thought of it first. "Where'd you get that?"

"Nowhere you'll ever see."

"Okay . . . " Jon let that disturbing information pass and said, "Talk to you later."

"Later." As Zane disconnected, Jon heard the alert for his messaging app.

All thoughts of marriage and tattoos fled. His contact—the ISIS recruiter—was reaching out.

With a shaky hand that belied his usual cool

demeanor, Jon hit the buttons to read the message.

Prepare. Travel instructions to follow.

Things were starting to move and Jon had to be one hundred percent ready.

He glanced at the closed bedroom door. Inside that room slept the woman he was going to have to leave without explanation.

Clenching his jaw he strode, determined, toward the bedroom.

His travel instructions most likely wouldn't come in the next half hour or so and too bad if they did. He wasn't going without loving Ali one more time before he left.

If things went south, it could possibly be the final time they'd be together ever.

He turned the knob and pushed the door open, closing it quietly before walking as silently as he could across the carpeted room.

Being stealthy was kind of pointless since he had every intention of waking her, but he'd rather do it with his kiss than the slam of a door. Hopefully, she'd be more receptive to the disruption to her sleep that way.

He slid beneath the sheets and across the wide bed until he was pressed against her warm body. He ran his hands over her curves and couldn't silence the groan that escaped from his throat.

Brushing his lips over her mouth in the dim light of dawn, he pushed the hem of her nightshirt up and over her hips.

She drew in a breath as she woke. "What are you doing?"

"Making love to you." Rolling on top of her, he

pressed one of his knees between her legs and further proved his intention.

Wrapping her arms around his neck, she whispered, “Okay.”

God, he was going to miss her.

CHAPTER EIGHT

Ali woke to brilliant sunlight streaming through the window and an empty side of the bed where Jon should have been.

No surprise there. He was usually up before she was. Even when she had to work, it didn't require she get up as early as Jon usually woke.

The good news was he was so quiet when he got up she rarely heard him. He was like a ninja.

A ninja who'd made coffee.

She breathed in the aroma of the freshly brewed beverage that permeated the closed bedroom door.

The combination of the tantalizing smell and the fact Jon had been sweet enough to make coffee motivated her to get out of bed even though it was her day off and she technically didn't have to get up.

She shuffled toward the kitchen, where she found Jon and said, "Good morning."

"Good morning." He came forward and pulled her to him, pressing a quick kiss to her lips. "I'm glad you're up."

"Mm, and I'm glad you made coffee." She moved toward the cabinet.

"I got it." Reaching over her head, Jon took down a mug from the high shelf and handed it to her, saving her from having to balance on tiptoe and grab a handle with her fingertips.

"Thanks."

That was just one of the problems of being a petite woman in the home set up by a tall man.

When—if—he ever made a commitment to her, the location of the coffee mugs would be the first thing she'd change.

She was just filling the mug when she noticed Jon hovering. She turned to him and waited.

It didn't take long before he said, "So I've got this job for GAPS that's been kind of on hold but I think things are about to start moving on it."

It was more than what he usually told her about an upcoming job.

Sure, in the old days when the company was first beginning and their biggest job was working security for some rich people Jon wasn't quite so secretive. But now GAPS's jobs entailed government contracts so she rarely was allowed to know anything.

Sometimes she'd pick up tidbits after an assignment was over, but rarely before.

"Oh? Okay."

When he pressed his lips together, she waited for the other shoe to drop.

"Once it starts I won't be able to make contact. I don't know for how long, but it could be awhile."

Frowning, she turned to face him fully, mug in hand. "Jon, this isn't new."

"I know. I just wanted you to be aware. And not to worry."

She let out a snort. *Not worry. Sure.*

He tipped his head to the side, a small smile bowing his lips. "Okay, try not to worry too much."

"I'll try."

"Good." He pulled her into a tight hug. She had to grip her mug tighter and only hug him back with one arm.

When he moved back, cupped her chin and just gazed at her, she had to wonder what was up with him.

Finally, he pressed a long slow deep kiss to her lips before pulling away.

He took a step back and let out a breath. "I need to get going to the office and take care of a few things."

"Okay." She nodded.

She watched as he walked to the closet and emerged with the mysterious full duffle bag that had been located there since she'd known him.

He opened the front door and paused just inside to glance back. "I love you."

"I love you too."

After a second, he stepped outside, closing the door behind him.

Life with Jon had always been full of oddities. This morning's interaction only reinforced that. Though she had to wonder what had him acting extra peculiar today.

Whenever he got back they'd have to have a talk. If he was taking jobs with GAPS that were as dangerous as when he'd been a SEAL, they needed to discuss it.

He'd left the military, but it appeared from how he was acting he hadn't left any of the danger behind.

After that realization, she really was worried.

Sighing, she topped off her coffee, grabbed a banana from the counter and headed into the living room.

It had been a long time since she'd indulged in a pajama day. Today seemed like the perfect time to veg on the sofa in front of the TV all day long. She reached for the remote control and settled in for a day of self indulgence.

Many hours and an entire season of the show she was binge watching later the ringing of Ali's cell phone broke into her enjoyment of her Netflix marathon.

She hit pause on the show and reached for the phone . . . and frowned at the name on the caller ID.

Zane? That was odd. He didn't usually call her. Maybe Jon was with him and his battery was dead.

Only one way to find out. "Hello?"

"Hi, Ali. It's Zane. Sorry to bother you but Jon's not answering his cell. Is he with you?"

"No. I'm home alone. He left early this morning and told me to not worry if he didn't come home because of that GAPS assignment that's been on hold."

"What? What assignment?"

Ali was too annoyed with Jon's hours and GAPS in general to want to deal with this conversation or Zane now. Especially not in the middle of the season finale of the show she'd devoted the whole morning to.

She sniffed at his question. "Seriously? Come on, Zane. You know he doesn't tell me anything. You're his partner. Don't you know what assignments he's working on?"

"I thought I did but apparently not." The sound of Zane hitting keys loudly replaced his voice momentarily. "No emails or messages either."

It was oddly comforting that Jon was as elusive with his business partner regarding his comings and goings as he was with her.

"I don't know what to tell you. All I know is, he took that overnight bag he keeps packed with him."

"He took his go-bag?" Zane's shock was apparent in the rise in his volume.

Meanwhile, she wished these guys would remember she didn't speak military-ease. "I don't know what it's called. It's kind of like a duffle bag stuffed full with something and it's always in the closet by the front door."

Zane mumbled a cuss. "What else did he say?"

If she was going to be interrogated she might as well relax. This might take awhile. Ali flopped back onto the sofa and relayed word for word, step by step, her interaction with Jon that morning. When she was done, Zane let out an audible breath tinged with another obscenity. His reaction was starting to worry her.

"Zane, what's going on?" She hadn't been more

worried about Jon's work than usual, until this discussion with Zane. Now she was starting to panic.

If a fellow SEAL was upset about Jon's behavior, there had to be cause for concern.

He paused a beat before saying, "It's nothing, Ali. Just Jon being Jon. Trying to handle everything on his own and not keeping me in the loop. I'm sure it's just a run of the mill assignment he didn't want to bother me with while I'm in D.C.. It's just hard to be his partner when I don't know everything that's happening in the company, you know?"

She let out a short laugh. "Welcome to my world. Anyway, if I hear anything, I'll let you know."

"Thanks. I'll do the same."

"Thank you. I'll talk to you later then. Good bye—"

Zane had already disconnected by the time she finished saying the final word. That was typical Zane, immediately on to the next thing, she was sure.

These guys were all too intense. She had to wonder if the military made them that way, or if this type of man just gravitated to service on their own.

It was the old chicken and egg debate, and she wasn't going to solve it today.

She picked up the remote with the futile hope that the sticky situation the fictional characters on TV were in could distract her from her real life. At least for a little while.

CHAPTER NINE

"Tell me, why does an American want to fight for the Islamic State?" Abu Jamal Ahmad leaned against the beat-up vehicle and crossed his arms.

Beneath the blazing Turkish sun, Jon felt the full weight of the stare the man leveled on him.

In spite of the scrutiny, Jon remained calm and cool. "It's my understanding a lot of Americans have come to fight before me. I follow in their footsteps."

"True. But why do *you* want to be a holy warrior? A custodian of the one true faith? I'm told that you, Jon Smithwick, are a man who has fought and killed in the name of the crusader infidels." The man said the final two words—ISIS's description of the American government and military—like they left a bad taste in his mouth.

Schooled in tempering his expression, Jon didn't react to being addressed by the fake surname printed on his forged paperwork. He'd prepared long and hard to be able to be Jon Smithwick, without thought, without hesitation.

Jon had researched this. Studied the interviews with Americans who were radicalized. Their histories. Their motives. From all he'd read and heard, he'd concocted a backstory for himself—or rather for Jon Smithwick. A plausible reason why a man with time in the military would want to join ISIS.

"That's exactly why." He was Jon Smithwick now as he explained, with conviction, his reasons. "I have followed their every order for most of my adult life. I killed for them. Many have. But afterward, when they can no longer use us for their agenda, they abandon us with little or no support. They asked for my life and gave nothing in return. I've lost faith in the men running the military and the country I risked my life for."

The man who was to be his guide from Turkey to the Syrian border seemed pleased by the answer. Jon could see that clearly in his expression.

One more obstacle between Jon and his end goal fell away.

"I've heard that before from Americans who come to fight with us. We see on your television and internet reports of men who were once great fighters for your country left to beg in the streets."

"Yes. It's true." Jon nodded agreeing with that reality while wishing it weren't true.

"We welcome a man of your expertise. In fact, because of your years in your military, they have changed our plans for you."

Change, in this case, was not good. "They?" Jon asked.

"Our—what you would call human resources department. We can best make use of a man of your knowledge to advise us how to combat those trying to retake control of the land the caliphate rightfully occupies."

Skipping over the shock of the fact ISIS had a human resources department, Jon's mind worked as he reviewed the clues as to where he might be sent.

Retake the land the caliphate rightfully occupies.

That could be Syria or Iraq.

"You were a soldier in the army, no?" the man asked, interrupting Jon's train of thought.

Jon's background for his false identity listed him as having served in the regular Navy. Not exactly a lie but not quite the truth. That Abu Jamal had mentioned the wrong branch of service could be a test. Or Jon could be paranoid.

"No. Not the Army. The Navy. I was a sailor." Trying to not look too concerned about the change in plans, Jon decided to ask a question of his own in hopes of getting the location out of his escort. "So I won't be going to Syria to learn and train?"

It was well known that new recruits had to go through three months of training, which is why Jon had come expecting to be away at least that long.

Three months during which no one except for a small handful of men in the organization who hired him would know where he was or what he was doing. Not Ali. Not Zane or Rick or Chris. Not his parents.

As far as he knew there wasn't even a paper trail

of this assignment or his whereabouts for anyone to follow should he go missing. And even if there was, it was wrong now because plans had changed.

"You are more valuable elsewhere. I think you don't require the physical training that our other fighters are in need of." Abu Jamal smiled as his gaze dropped down Jon's body.

Jon nodded his thanks even as he realized his error in planning.

Physically, he still looked like he did when he was in the Navy. He should have come here looking less like a SEAL and more like a man who enjoyed the sofa and beer too much since getting out of the military.

At least one thing he'd done to prepare for this assignment had worked out perfectly. Jon ran a hand over his face and felt the extreme length of the untrimmed beard he had grown in. It had come in nicely. He fit right in with the jihadists to whom facial hair was so important.

More than important actually. It was forbidden for males to shave their faces or to cut their hair. It was a symbol of their religious dedication.

Meanwhile his own beard and hair had gotten so long it had become nothing more than a hot annoyance for Jon.

Not to mention that Ali had really hated it . . .

Thoughts of her would derail him. As his stomach twisted he pushed all the memories of her back where they belonged, and firmly locked the door to that compartment in his mind.

He'd get the job done and get home. He was ready for this. He had cash in various currencies, not one but two burner phones and various forms of his fake ID, which included a picture showing him sporting full beard. That all had been provided by his government contact in the states.

The same men who had created an actual profile for his false identity, just in case ISIS had access to military records.

They had provided everything he would need except for a weapon.

Jon would have really liked to have had a weapon.

If the shit hit the fan, he'd just have to make do. He'd been trained well to improvise.

Good thing, since it appeared thanks to the jihad human resources department he'd be improvising his whole damn mission.

He dared to ask, "So if not to training, where are we going?"

"We are going to the city the caliphate controls in Iraq. Our enemies have set up a base near there that has become a nuisance. You will help us make them go away."

Even without him naming the city, Abu Jamal had narrowed down the choices of possible locations considerably for Jon. Fallujah or Mosul were his best guesses.

Iraq.

Jesus, this changed everything.

Jon wasn't going to Syria for the usual foreign fighter training. He wasn't going to be able to gather and bring home what he'd been sent to retrieve . . . mainly specific details about the way ISIS recruited.

He had hopes of gaining enough knowledge of leadership structure, location and travel routines to cut off the stream of foreign fighters being recruited and trained in Syria.

The best way to defeat an enemy was to know him well and Jon knew that in the past ISIS had sacrificed thousands of their recruits. They'd sent these fighters to be killed or maimed in battle seemingly without much tactical or strategic thought.

But that had been when recruitment was high.

Now, indications showed a greatly decreased influx of immigrant fighters. Possibly one reason why ISIS had switched to the *remain and expand* strategy, which was even more deadly to everyone around the globe.

Indoctrinate them, train them, and send them back to their own countries to cause havoc. They were the sleeper cells responsible for the attacks in Europe. They were the lone wolves staging mass shootings in the US.

But instead of gathering valuable intel to turn over to the three-letter US agency that had covertly hired him to help stem the tide of radicalization and recruitment, Jon would now be expected to provide the jihadists with American military secrets. Information his volatile hosts no doubt planned to use to hurt US-led coalition forces in Iraq.

Failing to do what the already paranoid and suspicious leaders of ISIS wanted could out him as a spy. There was no getting out of there alive should that happen.

Shit.

"Can I help with your baggage?" Like the front desk attendant at an upscale hotel, his escort made the polite offer as he eyed the single canvas duffle Jon carried.

This man embodied so many contradictions to what Jon had expected. He wasn't some starry-eyed youth, brainwashed to run toward his death and glory beneath the ISIS banner. Abu Jamal was a well-spoken and presumably educated middle-aged Muslim man who spoke perfect English.

"Thanks, but it's just this one. I can handle it."

"Then we shall go." As he began walking, the man turned to ask, "Do you speak any Arabic?"

Jon had picked up quite a bit in his years in the teams, but in this case, he thought it best to keep that fact to himself. "No. Will that be a problem?"

"Not at all. We have Arabic volunteers, interpreters who can translate for those *muhajireen*—foreign fighters—who speak French, Russian, Dutch, Spanish, and of course, American." Looking pleased and proud of his organization, Abu Jamal grinned.

"Impressive." Jon forced a smile but felt anything but relieved by ISIS's international capabilities and infrastructure. Or the wide array of foreign volunteers willing to martyr themselves for the Islamic State.

So many men from so many countries, all who in some misguided act they thought was noble, willingly sought out ISIS for training in how to best kill and spread terror.

But Jon had to remember it was that very ISIS infrastructure as well as the thousands of men who had come before him that made it possible, almost easy, for him to come here. He'd just have to use their own organization against them.

"Yes, I suppose it is impressive. And we are finding the internet to be most useful. We can educate and train fighters while they remain in their own countries. In the comfort of their own homes. They need not even come here."

Jon nodded as his blood ran cold at the thought. How many more thousands had been recruited online? How many hundreds, possibly thousands of sleeper cells were there around the world, lying in wait to strike?

Seemingly satisfied, Abu Jamal pushed off the car he'd been leaning against and reached for the door handle. "Get in. We must go. We have long to travel before curfew."

Jon moved to the other side, tossing his bag on the floor before sliding inside himself.

ISIS was wealthy, but the car they would be traveling in was old, likely to not attract attention. It was a tactic the US operators often used while in hot zones on foreign soil. The engine would be in top shape but the worse the outside of the vehicle appeared, the better.

"Do you smoke cigarettes?" Abu Jamal paused to ask as he reached for the ignition.

"No, I don't."

He nodded. "Good. It is forbidden.

Torture. Kill. Rape. Terrorize. But don't smoke or stay out past curfew. Jon was truly down the rabbit hole now.

CHAPTER TEN

ISIS was nothing if not organized.

That had been apparent from the time he'd first approached the organization through social media while he was still in the US, and it was still true through his guided travels across countries and borders here in the Middle East to where he was now, an ISIS camp in Iraq.

An undisclosed camp in an unknown city since they'd covered his head *for his own safety* for the final leg of the trip.

He was sticking with the educated guess that he was at a camp somewhere just outside of the city of Mosul, ISIS's Iraqi capital.

That was actually a good thing since the US was supporting the Iraqi and Kurdish forces in northern Iraq in preparation to retake the city from ISIS.

Possibly just miles away there were US troops. That knowledge kept Jon sane through his daily dose of Islamic State indoctrination and all the fanatical teachings they tried to drill into his head.

Mind games were ISIS's specialty. This was evidenced by the fact Jon's passport was now in the hands of the jihadists so-called human resources department, no doubt to make him feel dependent upon them.

He understood how ISIS thought as an organization. How they operated. Fear must be maintained to control people. Taking the passport of all the new arrivals reinforced that fear. That control.

This tactic wasn't going to work on him for a few reasons. Mainly because the passport was a fake. A good fake, an untraceable fake, but a fake nonetheless.

With or without the passport for his alias Jon Smithwick in ISIS's hands, this assignment was going to go one of two ways. Either they'd figure out he was a US government plant or they wouldn't.

Neither scenario was particularly good, because even if he managed to maintain his cover they could still decide he was too valuable to let go and want him to stay.

Both cases would require an escape on his part.

If only he'd been sent to Syria for training as planned. Then they would have returned him to his home after three months to spread the word and plan his own attacks.

As it stood, with him instead going through just basic indoctrination for the past couple of weeks in Iraq, he wasn't sure what the plans were for his future.

Maybe he was to be a permanent fixture here, advising them on all things American military. He didn't know.

What he did know was that he was on his own, which is why he spent his days and sometimes his nights planning. Studying protocols and procedures. Observing personnel movements. Searching for weaknesses. Holes in the security. Holes in the fences too—literally.

Memorizing every detail of the camp. Never knowing what might aid his escape if—when—the time came.

It wasn't hard to observe the camp since his days there were long and active. Life there wasn't all that different from his time in the Navy. He'd been in that military regimen for well over a decade and he fell easily back into a regimented existence now.

He was used to this. Memorizing the information they learned in the classroom setting. Excelling at the demands of the physical training. One thing that was completely different, however, was his lack of a weapon and body armor. He felt that absence keenly through every night and every day.

Some of the men there weren't as good at keeping up with the mental or physical requirements.

Jon spotted the weaker ones immediately and steered clear, taking his own performance down a notch when necessary. Outdoing the others would make him stand out when that was the last thing he wanted to do. It might also foster resentment and he didn't plan on making enemies of the other fighters.

The reality was that what Jon had couldn't be

taught. It wasn't immodest to think that. It was fact. Things like superior situational awareness, quick reflexes and good coordination meant the difference between a fighter being good enough or great.

Training and practice could impart a limited amount of skill to those not born with it, but to be a great fighter required inborn skills that were then honed through training and practice.

Then there was having guts. Balls. Courage. The fight versus flight instinct. Whatever. The best fighters had the innate urge to run toward danger rather than away.

Most of the men Jon had seen here had come to ISIS without the necessary inherent skills to be great fighters.

He knew because since no one talked to him he was left alone most of the time to study and observe the others. Language was one barrier. Jealousy and competition another. But that was fine with him. He hadn't come there to make friends.

Most of the men he trained alongside would be expendable in an attack. Pawns in this chess game they'd chosen to join. Used to swell the ground numbers and impress an enemy. Employed as cannon fodder to keep the opposition busy and distract eyes from the organization's greater aims.

The low quality of the recruits wasn't a surprise. Terrorist organizations didn't recruit from the larger diverse members of the mainstream population. They drew from the disgruntled few who lived on the edges of society.

And for their foreign fighters, ISIS often reached their candidates by using the web.

But it wasn't enough to hope to catch a few lone wolves as they were recruited via social media. They needed to go after the Islamic source of radicalization.

That was the very reason Jon had come. He only hoped his time in Mosul would be as lucrative—intelligence-wise—as his time in a training camp in Syria would have been.

He certainly was busy. Reveille was at zero-five-thirty followed by an hour-long workout. After that were lessons until lunchtime and then a scheduled rest for a couple of hours before the training continued until seventeen-thirty.

It was a grueling schedule for some, but a twelve-hour day with a ridiculously long mid-day break seemed like a vacation compared to some of the training he'd endured in his military career.

Most of the fighters there wouldn't have made it through the first day of BUD/S, never mind making it through the seven-day stretch aptly known as Hell Week.

Jon's thoughts were interrupted by Abu Jamal, striding toward him. When he was close, he said, "Greetings, Warrior."

Amused by what had become his nickname, Jon couldn't help a small smile. "Greetings, Abu Jamal."

"You did well today."

Jon dipped his head to accept the compliment. "Thank you."

"How do you excel so far beyond the others?"

Shit. Time to tone things down more.

Since he couldn't admit to being in top shape

because he'd gone right from a SEAL team to an elite private military company with government contracts that tested his metal all over the globe, he pawed through his brain for a diversion.

He remembered one of his instructor's golden rules for combat effectiveness. It would work perfectly now. "I learned long ago to train how I fight and fight how I train."

The man narrowed his eyes as he digested Jon's words, finally slowly nodding. "Wise. Please forgive me when I claim that as my own in tomorrow's teachings."

Jon smiled. "Please do. I got that wisdom from one of my own teachers."

He returned Jon's smile. "We are truly blessed to have you."

Words like that would go far to please many of the recruits and Jon began to see how ISIS retained loyalty. They wooed those looking for guidance. For praise.

Unfortunately for his ISIS mentor, the words failed to win over Jon. But for now, in the face of his teacher's compliment, Jon pretended to be one of those recruits hungry for praise from his leader.

"Thank you, Abu Jamal. You do me great honor in saying so."

"I think it's time."

"Time?" Jon braced himself for an answer he didn't want to hear. Something like, *time to strap on this suicide belt.*

Jon's skillset happened to include disarming bombs—at least the simpler ones—so that part wouldn't be a problem.

But his cover would be the only thing blown when he didn't blow up. Then he'd have to arrange for his own exfil because they would no doubt kill him for betraying them.

Of course, no one had said this would be easy.

Jamal finally ended Jon's guessing game of worst case scenarios by saying, "Time to meet Abu Salah."

In the ever revolving door of leadership resulting from deaths caused mostly by US airstrikes, it was hard to keep track of who was currently in charge of what in the organization, but after months of study and weeks here Jon had basically figured out the hierarchy.

As far as Jon could tell Abu Salah was acting as the minister of war for ISIS in Iraq.

There was something else Jon had gathered in his observations—Salah was not the highest ranking jihadist in camp. From things that were said he'd gathered there was someone higher Salah reported to.

From the twenty-four hour guards stationed outside an off-limits building in camp, Jon had a strong feeling where this person was. The only question that remained was *who* it was.

His best guess was that it was the organization's second in command, Abu Ala-Afri, aka Abd al-Rahman Mustafa al-Qaduli.

Jon had studied the man who was in the top five of the list of Islamic State leaders with targets on their backs. He was a brilliant strategist, a former teacher, and a charismatic preacher. Most importantly, he was Iraqi.

Mosul was his home. He'd trained under Osama Bin Laden. Even with the seven million dollar bounty on al-Qaduli's head, it made sense to have the local here. He knew the area. He would be more helpful running operations from Mosul rather than in hiding somewhere in Syria.

It didn't make Jon feel any confidence that the jihadist leaders on every US kill list could be there in the same camp where he was. It meant he was in danger of being killed by a US drone strike, as well as being beheaded by ISIS for being a spy.

But again, if this job were easy, everyone would do it.

Yeah, not so much.

Inside the office Jamal had led him to, Jon drew in a breath and bowed his head before Abu Salah.

"Ah, finally I meet the one they call Warrior." Abu Salah gestured to a chair. "Please, sit."

Silently, Jon did as told, not sure it was in his best interest to have that name following him around camp. Especially not when it came to leadership and their growing expectations of him. So much for his plan to remain under the radar as much as possible . . .

After a tip of Abu Salah's head, Abu Jamal backed out of the room, leaving Jon alone with the leader.

The long silent stare that followed had Jon feeling like the man was trying to peel back his skin and see inside his soul.

A man not trained as well as Jon might have begun to panic from the scrutiny. The fact was Abu Salah's tactics didn't even make Jon break a sweat.

Was this Salah's idea of acting tough? Being intimidating? Yeah, this wasn't gonna do it.

Although Jon should probably act like he was afraid. Best to keep the leaders happy by feeding their overinflated opinions of themselves.

"I'm honored to be in your presence, Abu Salah." Jon realized it wasn't exactly groveling, but it should stroke the man's ego.

A slow tip of Salah's head wasn't his only response to Jon's homage. He seemed to beam with his own self importance.

Jon would truly enjoy taking this man down. Or at least be one cog in the wheel that would. The information he would turn over when he got back could go a long way in helping destroy this camp and the leadership within it.

When he got back . . . Random thoughts such as that one always brought Ali to mind. No matter how hard he worked to not think about her, she was always there. In his mind. In his heart. Reminding him he had something to survive for.

That gave him strength while at the same time made him weak. He couldn't let thoughts of home—of her—affect him. His life literally depended on it.

"Tomorrow after morning exercises and the classroom teachings, you will come here."

The change in routine immediately put Jon on edge. "So I am to come here instead of physical training with Abu Jamal?"

"You have trained enough, Warrior. Now it is time for you to educate us."

Crap.

CHAPTER ELEVEN

Darci had just opened the front door when Ali couldn't contain her anger or her tongue any longer.

She stalked past Darci and into the house, ranting as she stomped. After dumping her purse on a chair, she spun back to Darci. "Weeks. Do you realize Jon has been gone for weeks?"

Her friend didn't deserve her bad mood, but since the real object of her frustration was nowhere to be found, Darci had become the target by default.

"Um, yeah. I guess I did know." Darci closed the door and walked to where Ali stood near the kitchen island. "You still haven't heard from him?"

"No! I've gotten not one phone call or text or email or anything."

"I'm sorry, Ali. I can't believe he didn't get any word to you at all." Darci turned to Chris, who was sitting suspiciously quiet on the sofa.

His attention seemed completely glued to the TV. Since the show on screen was a cooking program, and not some manly chef either, it seemed extra odd. There was no way Chris was that enthralled by the snooty lady chef from New York who cooked for all her rich friends at her house on the beach.

Darci frowned at her fiancé. “Chris. Do you know anything?”

“Nope.” He shook his head and delivered that single definitive word firmly.

Eyes wide, Ali strode to the living room area. Darci beat her there. Together, they presented a united front as they stood between him and the television.

“You know something,” Darci accused.

Weeks of worry had Ali torn between anger and tears. “Chris, please. If you do—”

“I don’t. Ali, I swear to you on my momma’s life.”

“Then why are you acting so weird?” Darci asked.

Chris pressed his lips together before saying, “Because if Jon has gone dark it has to mean he’s involved in something big. It’s not like him that he disappeared without Zane or Rick or me knowing where he was going.”

Darci’s eyes flew wide. “So, what are you saying? You think he was kidnapped?”

“No. Why would you think that? He told Ali he had a job. He took his go-bag. He left under his own power, just in complete secrecy. At least as far as we’re all concerned.”

Darci folded his arms. “So what do you think is going on?”

Chris shrugged. “He must have taken a job on his own.”

“What kind of job?” As Darci fired the next question at Chris, Ali stood by and watched.

It felt a bit like a bad dream. Like she was an observer, outside the situation. Unable to talk. Frozen in place. Invisible to those in the room.

“I don’t know. He left no trail, no evidence of what it is or where he is. And believe me, I looked. I ripped that office apart, right down to searching the ceiling tiles and the vents.” Chris shook his head and finally turned his focus to Ali. “You a’ight?”

“No.” Ali shook her head. When she stopped the small motion, she realized the room hadn’t stopped swaying.

Stumbling, Ali reached for the arm of the chair.

Darci stepped forward. “Whoa. What’s wrong? Are you okay?”

Besides all the stuff with Jon stressing her out, she was now having fainting spells? Lovely. What the hell else could the universe throw at her? Hadn’t she already been going through enough?

“I’m fine. Just dizzy.”

“Sit down.” Darci guided Ali into the chair. “Have you eaten today?”

Ali frowned as she tried to remember. “Um . . .”

“If you have to think that hard about the last time you’ve eaten, then it’s been too long.” After that declaration, Darci spun toward Chris. “Chris—”

“I’m on it. I’ll run out and get something. What do want?”

“Chinese?” Darci asked Ali. “A nice eggroll and some hot soup? And some vegetable dumplings and beef and broccoli maybe?"

"Whatever you get is fine. Thank you."

Darci turned to Chris. He nodded as he reached for his keys on the counter. "Got it. Be back shortly."

"Thank you, baby."

"No problem, darlin'." Chris dropped a kiss on Darci's forehead before he was out the door.

Once they were alone, Darci's full attention was back on Ali. "I'll get you some water. Or maybe hot tea? Which do you want?"

Darci was a caretaker by nature. If she even got a whiff of the fact that someone wasn't feeling well she would be there with food and support.

After years of being her friend and coworker, Ali knew this. Ali also knew it was pointless to try and stop Darci from trying to help. It was just simpler and easier on everyone to let her fuss.

"Tea maybe. Thanks."

"I'll put the kettle on. Herbal or regular? Actually, if you're lightheaded, you should probably have herbal." Darci asked and then answered her own question.

"Okay." Whatever made Darci happy was fine with Ali.

As long as she stayed sitting and didn't move her head too fast, the room didn't spin and that was a good thing.

Darci was back in a couple of minutes. She sat on the sofa and leaned forward, eyeing Ali. "Just waiting for the water to boil. You feel any better?"

"A little." Ali bit her lip. While Darci had been in the kitchen, she'd had some time to think and she realized there was one thing that she'd been ignoring, but in light of the dizzy spell and the wave of nausea when Darci had mentioned greasy eggrolls, the thought niggled again at the back of her mind. "I'm late."

"Late for what?" Darci asked. "I don't think you should drive if you're dizzy."

"No, not late for an appointment." Ali let out a short laugh. If only that were the case. "I'm late for my period."

Darci widened her eyes. "Oh my God. You think you're pregnant? How? Aren't you on birth control pills?"

"Yes. And I've never missed taking them. Ever. So I don't know how I could be. You're right. That can't be it. It was stupid. It has to be the stress. That's what is making me late."

Darci's brow creased. "Are you taking anything that could interfere with the pill? Like prescription meds?"

"No. I mean I started taking St. John's Wort every day, but that's all natural."

"Ali, I remember reading something about that. Hang on." Darci jumped up to grab her laptop off the dining room table.

"I'm sure it's nothing. It's a plant for God's sake." Ali waved off Darci's concern.

"That doesn't mean anything. Even a bad drug like heroin starts out as just a flower." Darci's voice rose in tone and volume.

Ali rolled her eyes and waited, not believing an herbal supplement available on the shelves of any local store could render her prescription birth control ineffective. Surely there would be a warning label if that were true.

But when Darci sucked in a sharp breath, Ali started to worry. "What?"

"Holy cow. Ali, that stuff messes with birth control pills. Listen to this. 'There have been cases of unintended pregnancies in women taking St. John's Wort and birth control pills.'" As her eyes grew wide, Darci raised her gaze to stare at Ali.

Ali's heart pounded as the ramifications of what her friend had discovered hit her.

Her boyfriend was not only against marriage and having children, but he was also missing. There was no other word for her to use since she didn't know where Jon was and neither did his business partner.

And now she might be pregnant.

Alone and pregnant. Ali tried not to panic. She didn't know for sure yet, but her period was late. That she did know for certain. She'd need to buy a test.

God, she hoped this was a false alarm.

But what if it wasn't? The thought was too overwhelming. She'd have to force that worry out of her head because she couldn't deal with it now.

"What are you going to do?" Darci asked.

Ali drew in a bracing breath and met Darci's gaze. "I'm sure it's nothing. I'm positive I'm late because I'm so worried about Jon. Look it up. I bet stress messes up women's cycles."

"Yeah, it probably does but—"

"If I don't get it in a couple of days, I'll buy a test just to make sure. Okay?"

"How late are you?"

"Just a couple of days." Ali waved her hand to dismiss Darci's concern.

Or a week. Ali kept that internal count to herself.

Finally Darci and her narrow-eyed glare seemed satisfied with Ali's answer. She nodded. "Okay."

"Please don't tell Chris about any of this." The teakettle chose that moment to start to whistle. Darci got up to tend to it, which forced Ali to have to call after her. "Darci, promise me you won't tell Chris."

"I promise." She glanced back at Ali for barely a second before she focused on the kettle and Ali wasn't sure if she believed her friend or not.

The last thing she needed was for Chris to tell Jon about this. Then again, since no one could get in touch with Jon it didn't really matter, now did it?

It seemed both Jon and her period were missing in action.

Ali let out a sigh as the pile of her worries grew higher.

"Honey?" Darci asked, the little plastic honey bear held in her hand.

Even a mundane decision such as that seemed overwhelming when her life was completely upside down.

For lack of a real preference, Ali said, "Sure. Thanks."

CHAPTER TWELVE

Two truths and a lie.

Wasn't that the name of some sort of icebreaker game people played at parties? Jon was pretty sure it was.

If so, it was the game he was currently playing with Abu Salah, only the other man wasn't aware he was playing.

Jon fed him tidbits. About past US troop movements. Training protocols. Things that were true but pretty innocuous. Nothing that couldn't be found with a little digging on the internet. Definitely nothing that would risk American lives, but things that would lend credence to Jon's cover as a recruit dedicated to the Islamic State's cause.

The best way to lie was to put as much truth in it as possible.

But then Jon would throw a whopper of a lie in for good measure. Things he pretended to be privy to accidentally. From a drunk officer who had a big mouth at a bar near base. From a service member breaking OpSec and bragging.

Jon's one bright spot during the day was seeing Abu Salah's eyes widen at the tall tales. And if ISIS acted on the false rumors and it cost them time and money as they tilted at windmills, all the better. That would mean less resources they could use against the actual coalition forces.

That was how things went for the first few days in Jon's new position as the camp's chief source of information about their opposition. But today seemed different.

He felt it the moment he walked through the door. The energy coming off Salah was tangible. The man vibrated with excitement.

Something had happened or was about to.

"Good morning, my Warrior. Come, sit. We have much to discuss."

Much to discuss.

Jon's gut feeling had been dead on, right when he really wished it hadn't been. Something was up. Now he needed to know what—and what, if anything, he could do to stop it.

ISIS was willing and able to adapt quickly. They'd proven it repeatedly. It was something he'd always wished the US military was better at. But in spite of ISIS's quick pivots and abilities, he'd be damned if he let the organization hurt even one more person without doing everything he could to prevent it.

Even if he died trying.

Memories of the Paris and Brussels attacks sat in

the forefront of his mind as he asked, "Yes, Abu Salah?"

There was a knock on the door and Jon had the urge to kill whoever was outside interrupting Salah's answer to his question.

After he called for the intruder to come in, Abu Salah smiled. "Ah, good."

Jon twisted in the chair and got an eyeful of a man carrying a weapon and ammo. An American military weapon.

He drew in a breath to calm the anger of seeing up close what he'd already known—that when ISIS took control of this part of Iraq they also took control of the equipment the American's had supplied to the Iraqi army.

Salah jumped up from his seat and moved around to Jon's side of the desk. He lifted the machine gun and grinned wider. "Nice, no?"

"Very nice." Nice for ISIS. For the US? Not so much.

It was a US Army machine gun valued at approximately four thousand dollars new, and now in the hands of an ISIS leader.

Jon noticed Salah held the weapon awkwardly, like it was unfamiliar to him.

Hyper vigilance. Noticing even small things. It was Jon's legacy from years of deployments in a war zone where he had to expect the unexpected every second. It, among other things, were the skills that had kept him alive, and they'd stuck with him.

Today, noticing Salah was a novice in handling the weapon fueled Jon's courage and determination.

"You've used one before?" Salah asked.

Jon nodded. “Yes, I have.”

“Good. This one is yours.”

Jon felt his eyes go wide. “Mine?”

“Yes. You will accompany us on the attack.”

With a sick feeling in his gut, he asked, “What attack?”

“The one we shall make against the American dogs to our south.” With two hands, Salah thrust the weapon forward.

Jon took it. Just the feel of the weight in his hands brought a feeling of calm. Whatever happened, at least he’d be armed. He could work with that.

He raised his gaze to meet Salah’s. “When do we attack?”

The man met his comment with a smile. “Soon, Warrior. Very soon.”

Salah’s words haunted Jon for the remainder of the day. Through target practice with his new weapon where his accuracy blew away that of all the others alongside him. Through the afternoon rest and the evening meal.

Those words made falling to sleep that night nearly impossible.

Jon had too many questions with no answers. There was too much thinking to do for him to rest. How could he prevent an event he didn’t have nearly enough information about?

The answer didn’t come. Finally, as it usually did, exhaustion won out.

CHAPTER THIRTEEN

Jon didn't know how long it had been since he'd fallen into a fitful sleep in the fighters' barracks when he was roused from sleep.

The shouted instructions, delivered in a language he didn't speak but was familiar enough with to understand, instructed them to assemble in the courtyard.

He had the fleeting thought that they'd discovered his true purpose for being there. That he'd be the next beheading on the morning news.

That Ali and his parents would all have to watch—

He remembered the machine gun next to him on the mattress and pushed that thought aside. He wasn't helpless. If he had to, he'd go down fighting.

Since he'd slept in his clothes, Jon only needed to pull on his boots and grab the weapon and ammo.

Outside, he saw that Salah hadn't been lying

about the attack being soon. If the dozen Humvees, two Howitzers, and small army of fighters already assembled and outfitted with various weapons was any indication, this was happening tonight.

A familiar rumble had Jon turning and—*mother fucker*—an M1A1 Abrams tank padded slowly into view.

His heart pounded as Jon took in the scene of a well-equipped army about to go to battle, all while he stood on the wrong side of the line.

Equipment alone didn't make a fighting force. He reminded himself that it took well-trained men and Jon knew most of these men were not. He was though, and it struck him that in spite of that they were planning to throw him out there with the rest of the cannon fodder.

The very leaders who called him Warrior and lavished him with praise were going to sacrifice him along with the rest of these men in an attack that was probably going to result in massive casualties on this side.

He knew even if the jihadists did manage to surprise the US-led forces with this attack, it wouldn't take long for the allied forces' air support to arrive and mow them all down.

Jon supposed his less-than-esteemed leadership figured they'd gotten all the information they could out of him and he too was now expendable.

Maybe they thought he'd at least take out some of their enemies before he perished.

Or hell, maybe they thought he was some sort of superman and might actually make it out of this alive. It could be. They were bat-shit crazy, at best.

He didn't know what their motivation. But bruised ego aside, he had to be happy they were sending him on what amounted to a suicide mission because it would put him close enough to the action to hopefully do something about it.

Exactly what he could do was the question.

He'd racked his brain for a valid plan of action ever since Salah had dropped the bombshell about an attack without providing any details. But unlike earlier, Jon now had additional information.

As soon as they grew nearer to the point of attack, he'd have even more. Weapon in his hands, he loaded into the vehicle with as many of the other fighters as would fit inside and prepared for the unexpected.

Jon's mind spun with possibilities during the hour plus drive.

Makhmour.

That had to be where they were headed.

Jon had timed the drive so far and it was just about an hour. They'd traveled first due south before swinging to the east.

If his best guess was correct, they were smack in the middle of what was the Makhmour farming district—before ISIS arrived and changed the lives of the locals.

Now, the area was also the home of Fire Base Bell. A full company of US Marines occupied the fire base to provide force protection for the nearby Camp Swift, a US forward operating base set in the middle of the larger Kurdish Peshmerga camp.

It was a region Jon knew well. After one of the Marines had been killed by an ISIS rocket that struck inside the wire at the fire base, Jon and Zane had researched the hell out of the region. They'd put together a proposal for a GAPS team to assist the US military there.

ISIS had had enough information to stage an attack on the Marines before the rest of the American public, which included Jon and Zane, were aware the newly created fire base even existed.

That wasn't such a surprise actually. When the US had first entered Afghanistan small outposts were thrown up with little notice from anyone except for the troops building the fire base and the Taliban enemy observing them.

This wasn't ten years ago in Afghanistan. This was today in Iraq, and the coalition had already fought for and won Fallujah and Ramadi and Mosul—before ISIS.

ISIS in Mosul was a problem Jon had hoped GAPS could help solve.

The camp Fire Base Bell was set up to protect was home to Iraqi and Kurdish Peshmerga troops, as well as US advisory forces. Those included US Navy SEALs, if the information Zane had about the most recent casualty was correct.

The review committee hadn't agreed to let GAPS come here months ago, and they wouldn't even take Zane's request for a meeting now.

Just one of the many reasons Jon had agreed to take this assignment. If GAPS couldn't help through official channels, Jon would in ways that were a little . . . less official. He could get more accomplished like this than with the government and the military looking over his shoulder anyway.

Inside one of the Humvees, squashed shoulder to shoulder with two men who didn't speak English, he realized he would never have had this kind of backstage pass to an ISIS attack had he come here as an advisor on a GAPS contract.

He could only hope he lived long enough to pass on all he'd learned to the organization that had sent him in. But first he had to either stop this attack or get word to the good guys it was coming.

The last thing he wanted was to be on the ISIS side of the line when air support swooped in, but if he couldn't sneak away that was exactly what would happen.

Sneaking away before the attack would be the best course of action. Breaking away might not be all that hard.

The quickly assembled attack unit was sloppy at best, comprised of fighters not all that concerned about discipline and leaders who valued quantity over quality.

Jon snapped to attention when the lead vehicle in the caravan stopped and the rest followed. They must be close to the line and they were stopping to plan and regroup.

In that most recent attack near Erbil, ISIS had crashed through a Kurdish checkpoint with armored vehicles and had barreled directly into the small town where the US advisors had been meeting with locals.

Jon had to think they wouldn't deviate much from what had proven to be a successful offense for them. Successful if they didn't consider that air support took out most of their fighters later that day. But it seemed the Islamic State treated fighters as an expendable, renewable resource so they probably didn't care how many they lost.

That this was a predictable enemy worked in his favor and as the entire convoy ground to a stop somewhere that had to be very near where he needed to be, Jon liked his odds.

Jumping down from the Humvee, weapon in hand, Jon took in his surroundings.

Chaos was a good word for the situation around him. Abu Salah emerged from a vehicle, shouting in Arabic to the troops in an attempt to organize the fighters.

They fell into a formation, Jon among them. Slouching to hide his height, he forced himself to blend in rather than stand out.

Once he imitated the stance of the other fighters, it was easy. They all wore the same black clothing and they'd all been supplied with a black hood for the attack. Looking the part was apparently more important to the leaders than actually having qualified men.

Jon stood as instructions were relayed in Arabic. Then the translators broke off from the group and repeated the information—in French. In Russian. In Belgian.

Finally, Abu Jamal approached to personally deliver Jon's instructions in English. "Warrior. Walk with me."

Jon tipped his head and followed the man to the edge of the light provided by the temporary encampment. Then Jamal continued into the darkness. There was a brief moment of doubt as to why he had been separated from the group.

Was this it? Had he been compromised?

The sound of Jamal unzipping the fly of his pants was followed shortly by the man's sigh as he relieved himself.

Jon wasn't going to be killed. Jamal just had to take a piss.

He let himself breathe again.

"Long drive," Jamal said.

"Shorter than I expected actually," Jon replied.

Abu Jamal let out a snort. "Yes, the Americans dare to set up a camp this close to us. Just a few miles from where we stand is the checkpoint where Kurdish dogs think they can keep us at bay. But we will show them."

"When? When do we attack?" Jon kept his voice steady even as his heart thundered at the turn of events.

He couldn't have asked for a better opportunity. Alone in the dark with Jamal. Just miles from the Kurdish check point. And he was about to have the last detail he needed. The answer to the one remaining question.

When.

"Just before first light." Abu Jamal supplied that final answer Jon needed.

Of course. They would have to wait until closer to dawn. The coalition forces had night vision equipment. Heat detection. The ability to see targets even in the dark. With night vision goggles, darkness was a friend.

But ISIS, for all they had stolen, was not so well

equipped. They needed the first light of dawn for the fighters to see. More importantly, the wait until dawn would give Jon all the time he needed.

Abu Jamal continued as he zipped his pants, "Abu Salah gave me a message for you, Warrior. Bring him back a hostage, preferably an American, and you may have the honor of taking the man's head. It is quite an honor for you."

The words sent a chill down Jon's spine, even as his anger sent the blood rushing through his veins. Before Jamal could turn back to camp, Jon made his move.

Swift and strong, Jon had him in a headlock in one quick smooth move.

While Jon choked him out, Abu Jamal managed to say, "I should have known."

As Jamal's body grew heavy against Jon's, he considered Jamal's gasped, muffled observation. He couldn't really disagree on that point. The signs had all been there that Jon was a professional fighter.

Jon answered Jamal, though by then he was probably past hearing. "Yeah, you should have."

Abu Jamal's mistake would cost him. Jon dispatched with his enemy quickly and silently with one twist and snap of his neck.

Chances were good no one would even notice Jon was gone but they might notice Jamal missing.

Shaking as the adrenaline surged through him, Jon flung the dead weight of Jamal's body over his shoulder and carried him deeper into the darkness. Far enough away that no one from the camp would stumble upon him should they need to similarly relieve themselves.

With that move buying him time to get away and to the checkpoint Jon dumped Jamal on the ground and then faded into the shadows of the night.

He ran full out, as fast as he could in the darkness lit only by stars and the smallest sliver of moon. Adrenaline and training made it so his gun and ammo were barely a noticeable weight as he quickly covered the few miles.

When the lights of the checkpoint came into view, he knew he had a choice to make. Put down his weapon—his best defense—and walk into the checkpoint with his hands up, or keep the gun and risk having the good guys shoot him for being armed.

He was, after all, coming at them from ISIS-held territory dressed like a jihadist.

Thank God he didn't sound like the typical ISIS fighter.

Laying the weapon down, Jon drew in a bracing breath and yelled, first in English and then in his passible Kurdish as well as in fairly decent Arabic, "I'm American. Don't shoot!"

It was the one phrase he knew in nearly every language.

With his gun in the dirt behind him and his hands held high in the air as he walked, he only hoped the words worked to protect him now.

CHAPTER FOURTEEN

How any doctor could think that a piece of paper masquerading as a gown was enough to make an otherwise naked patient feel covered and comfortable was beyond Ali. But she had plenty of time to contemplate the point as she sat on the edge of the table and stoically ignored the stirrups on either side of her while she waited . . . and waited.

What was taking the doctor so long anyway?

She was sure her blood pressure was getting higher the longer she sat there.

It had been bad enough the nurse had weighed her and written down what Ali knew was the heaviest she'd ever been in her life. But now the doctor was probably going to make a comment on her elevated blood pressure too.

Finally, the door swung open and Doctor Meredith Bergman came through. Young. Pretty. Thin. Tall. If the doctor weren't so damn friendly and nice, Ali would have really resented her.

It wasn't the doctor's fault she had flawless porcelain skin and hair like gleaming golden silk. It was, however, her fault she'd kept Ali waiting so long that she now felt like she was going to hyperventilate.

The doctor laid the chart on the counter and turned to Ali. "So, according to the test results, you were right."

"About what?" Ali swallowed hard, hoping she had been right about something else, instead of what she feared she'd been right about.

Doctor Bergman smiled. "You're pregnant."

Ali felt the room sway. "You're sure?"

"Yes, ma'am. I'm going to need to take a blood sample just to make sure your hormone levels are where they should be."

Ali barely felt as the doctor held her arm and siphoned out a tube of her blood. Normally the sight would have turned her stomach. Today, her stomach already churned but she was in too much shock to care.

She'd convinced herself her period was late from stress. It had been a good excuse. She'd liked that reason. Liked it so much she'd put off taking the home pregnancy test for days after she suspected she should have.

When she finally did, that little plus sign appeared on the stick and she couldn't put off making the appointment with her doctor any longer.

Even then, she'd held tight to her hope that the test had given a false positive. Maybe even because of that damn St. John's Wort she'd been taking.

But hearing it definitively from the OB/GYN dissolved that last bit of hope.

With the reality of a baby facing her, Ali was having trouble breathing. The doctor noticed and asked, “Are you all right?”

“Yeah. It’s just a shock.” Ali raised her eyes to meet the doctor’s concerned gaze. “I’ve been on the pill for almost two years.”

“Yes. It’s rare but it’s been known to happen. Obviously stop taking the birth control immediately if you haven’t already.”

Ali nodded and swallowed hard, worried because she hadn’t stopped taking the pills until after she’d taken the test. “Will it be okay? The baby, I mean?”

“It shouldn’t affect the baby but we’ll keep a close eye on things. And I recommend you stop taking the St. John’s Wort and any other herbal remedies you might have forgotten to list.” The doctor glanced at the chart and back up.

Point taken. She had done this to herself by trying to self medicate. Unknowingly, but even so, she’d made this bed and now she had to lie in it.

Lie in it alone apparently since she still couldn’t get in touch with Jon even if she had wanted to tell him about the baby, which she really didn’t.

God. This was an absolute disaster. Jon hadn’t even wanted to talk about the future for just the two of them, so she was pretty sure having an unexpected baby was not going to be on his *to do* list.

“Are you sure you’re feeling okay?”

Ali rallied every last bit of strength she had left in her and forced a smile. “Yeah. I’m fine.”

She managed to maintain the façade through the remainder of the appointment, but by the time she paid her insurance co-pay and made an appointment for the first of her prenatal visits, Ali was drained. She drove home in a daze.

Truth be told she probably shouldn't have been driving at all. Her mind wasn't on the traffic but she somehow made it to Jon's condo without incident.

Jon's condo. It was where she'd been living since the lease on her place had ended but it still felt like his—not *theirs*. Here, she kind of felt like a guest who'd overstayed her welcome.

Ali suddenly missed her old rental. It hadn't been that great—not like Jon's tricked-out, state of the art place with the automatic lights and security system worthy of Fort Knox—but it had been truly hers.

The confirmation of the pregnancy had drained her of all energy and will. She certainly didn't have the brainpower to contemplate her current living situation, or if she should change it.

It was all she could do to kick off her shoes and dump her purse on the counter. She locked the door but after a weary glance at the keypad didn't turn on the alarm. It seemed beyond her at the moment.

Besides, Jon wasn't there to yell at her about it anyway so . . .

Ali went directly to the sofa and flopped back on the pillow. She didn't even bother grabbing the remote control from the coffee table. There had to be hundreds of channels available to watch but she couldn't think of a thing that would take her mind off this.

Laying her hand over her belly, she felt the rounded mound beneath her fingers. Stress combined with Ben & Jerry's ice cream had been the main contributor, but now she knew Jon had had a little something to do with it too.

She felt the tears fill her eyes and yanked her hand off her stomach, transferring it quickly onto the sofa cushion next to her as if that would make it all go away. She let out a snort, knowing it wouldn't.

On the bright side, she finally had one reason to be glad Jon had disappeared without a trace. As long as he was gone, she wouldn't have to tell him the bad news.

Bad news. No baby should be considered that.

She moved her hand back to rest on her abdomen when she realized what she'd thought. "Sorry, baby."

Sighing, Ali dropped her head back against the cushion and closed her eyes. Worrying wouldn't change or solve anything.

Maybe a nap would.

Ali didn't know how long she'd been out before she was jarred awake.

She opened her eyes to find the living room completely dark except for the dim light coming through the window from the streetlights outside.

As her brain started to work a little better, it finally registered what had startled her awake. Someone was knocking on the door.

Pounding was a better word really.

Jon's safety lessons were ingrained in her. She moved toward the door and put one hand up to the alarm keypad, just in case.

Pushing the panic button was the best she could do if someone tried to force their way inside, since she hadn't armed the security system.

Even while he was absent she could imagine Jon's disappointment and judgment over that move.

One glance through the peephole had her letting out a loud frustrated breath. It was Darci and Chris.

Ali used two hands to unlock the deadbolt and open the door.

"What are you pounding about?" she asked as she stepped back and let them into the condo.

"Why don't you answer your cell phone?" Darci's eyes were wide as she countered with a question of her own while Chris closed the door behind him.

"I didn't hear it." Ali frowned and then remembered she'd put it on vibrate in the waiting room at the doctor's office so it wouldn't ring in the middle of her visit. It was still in her purse so of course she didn't hear it as she slept. "What's so urgent?"

Darci glanced at Chris. That move alone was enough to have Ali's heart pounding.

"What? Tell me."

It was Chris who answered. "They found Jon."

Found.

She'd waited for weeks for word on Jon but *found* was not the word she wanted to hear.

Found how? His body? Him alive? Him injured?

So many questions that Ali never got an answer to as the room swayed around her.

The last thing she saw was Chris reaching out to

grab her as she fell, while Darci shrieked. Then her vision dissolved into black.

CHAPTER FIFTEEN

Camp Swift, the US camp marked only by a hand painted wooden sign, was located in the middle of the larger ramshackle Kurdish military base.

The understated facility belied its importance. It was positioned perfectly for joint forces ground troops to operate out of in the effort to retake Mosul and defeat ISIS in northern Iraq.

Considering how critical the location, the camp was not impressive by any stretch of the imagination . . . and Jon had never been so happy to see any place in his life.

That had been true two hours ago when the Kurds had brought him here, even with his hands bound behind his back.

It remained true now, even as the senior American commander in Makhmour stood screaming at him so violently the spit from the force of his words had already hit Jon in the face and chest a few times.

At least Jon had been taken to the top guy at camp. That was something.

"You private contractor assholes think you can come over here and be some kind of a hero! And then when the shit hits the fan you expect us to swoop in with our men and our equipment and rescue you. Well, you're not going to pull this bullshit in my warzone. I will not put one US life on the line to save the likes of you or any of your friends. Since you're lucky enough, by some miracle, to be alive, you go home and tell all your Rambo buddies that."

He didn't remind the officer that he hadn't needed any rescuing. He'd made it to the Kurdish checkpoint without incident all on his own, without any help from him or his men or his equipment.

This wasn't the first dressing down he'd gotten from a superior officer. Since GAPS often worked in theater with US military, it probably wouldn't be his last.

Jon stared straight ahead, and took the accusations without comment while standing at *parade rest*.

It was the one standing military position he could do with his hands still zip-tied behind his back. He had a feeling the angry commander in front of him needed the reminder that Jon had once been a decorated sailor, no matter what he looked like now.

The first thing Jon was going to do when they cut him loose was shave this damn beard and trim his hair. He had enough of looking like a terrorist. It might have helped him while in the ISIS camp, but the look wasn't doing him any favors now.

"Do you understand?" the colonel asked. More like shouted in the way that officers always seemed to have down pat.

"Yes, sir."

The commander's brows rose. "You act like a member of the US military, but you sure as fuck don't look like one."

"No, sir."

"And tell me why that is?"

"I needed to keep up the appearance that I was an ISIS recruit."

"All while you were secretly working for some US entity that you refuse to identify."

"Yes, sir."

That answer brought about another colorful tirade of cursing.

"I should toss you in the brig and throw away the key." The man paced across the room and back again before saying, "No. You know what? I should give you back to your Daesh friends. Would you like that?"

"No, sir."

The man drew in a breath. He seemed out of things to say, though Jon wasn't going to count on that as the commander stood staring at the piece of paper on his desk and shaking his head.

"A fucking SEAL. And SEAL Team Six to boot. Of course. You guys all think you don't have to play by our rules. That you're too good. That you're *special*." He'd said that last word in a mocking tone of voice that showed exactly what he thought.

It seemed this man felt about SEALs pretty much the same as he felt about private military contractors. Jon remained silent and let him get it all off his chest.

He had yet to resort to using the emergency phone number Hasaan had provided. He would if he had to but for now, Jon had chosen to only give them his real name and social security number. They'd looked him up—obviously since the commander was currently sneering at a printout of Jon's service record.

Jon wished the commander would concentrate more on the ISIS fighters waiting for dawn to break through the checkpoint and a little less about his credentials.

He could yell at Jon all he wanted to later—after they sent in air support.

He'd given them all the details about the attack. Weapons. Numbers. The attack force's location as best as he could determine it. What he didn't have was the answer to what they'd done with that information.

There was only one way to find that out. "Sir?"

"What!" The colonel barked out the single word.

"Have you been able to confirm my information about the impending attack—"

"Oh, we're looking into that, boy. And you'd better hope we find your little attack force or you're going to be in even deeper shit than you are now."

Jon wouldn't have called the ISIS force he'd seen *little* but he didn't correct the commander. He was simply content they had taken his warning seriously enough to investigate further. When they did, they'd confirm the number of vehicles and fighters for themselves.

A knock on the door didn't end the commander's rant. It only refocused it for a moment as he yelled in the direction of the entry, "Come in!"

A lower ranking soldier opened the door and hovered there, as if deciding if it was safe to enter and more importantly, if the commander's wrath was going to be directed full force at him for interrupting.

"Well? What?" the commander barked when the soldier took too long to explain his presence.

"We've got visual confirmation of a force of men and vehicles two clicks from the check point, sir."

Good thing Jon had been well schooled in maintaining a straight face and was able to keep his extreme satisfaction from showing.

Judging by the commander's scowl, an *I told you so,* even communicated by just a facial expression and not in actual words, wouldn't have gone over too well right now.

The commander let out a huff and tipped his head toward Jon. "Cut him loose."

The subordinate did as told and Jon was finally able to move his numb arms after hours of confinement.

He rolled his shoulders and rubbed his wrists, but his mind had already moved on to the next step. "What can I do to help, sir?"

"Help? You want to help?" The commander sneered.

"Yes, sir. I was with those men for weeks. I

know their strengths and their weaknesses, their leadership structure, their equipment. I've seen how they think. How they act. How they train. I can help."

The commander bit out a foul curse and then drew in a deep breath. "Fine. You can come to the operations center, but dammit you'll speak only when spoken to. And after this clusterfuck is over, you're right back in hot water for being here in the first place. You understand?"

That was good enough for him. All he'd wanted to do was help in this fight. Thanks to the past few weeks, he was uniquely equipped to do so.

"Yes, sir." Jon nodded and followed the commander as he stalked out the door.

He'd win this man over yet or end up in the brig trying.

CHAPTER SIXTEEN

Defeating the group of fighters amassed on the edge of the ISIS held territory proved to be ridiculously easy, thanks to the information and prior warning the coalition forces had to work with.

Drones, satellite images, air support and a little inside knowledge from Jon had meant certain victory for the coalition.

Jon was sure Abu Salah must be most unhappy back in Mosul after hearing about the defeat, not to mention the losses of both men and machines. What equipment hadn't been destroyed in the attack was back in coalition hands, where it belonged.

The Kurdish forces were especially happy to take the risk and raid the battlefield after the fact for anything they could salvage. They came back to camp driving slightly battered Humvees filled with scavenged weapons, while sporting the biggest smiles Jon had seen since he'd arrived there.

Even the commander was in a good mood, in spite of Jon's presence. Such a good mood, Jon took a chance and asked, "Sir, would I be able to contact my business partner in the states?"

Jon might need Zane's Washington D.C. contacts to get him out of this mess if the commander made good on his threats of disciplinary action.

"Your business partner. And what is he going to be able to do for you? Hmm?"

Time for some name dropping. "I thought maybe he and our majority investor, Senator Greenwood, might want to know where I am."

That spurned another round of cursing from the commander, which didn't surprise Jon a bit. What did surprise him was when, shaking his head, the commander laughed. "You know what, Rudnick? I really want to hate your guts. You and your senator friends and your private company make it real easy. And then you go and aid us in running the smoothest operation against Daesh I've seen since stepping foot in this God forsaken place. So now I have to respect you. And that pisses me the fuck off."

Jon allowed himself a small smile. "Yes, sir. I know."

The commander waved an arm in the direction of the door. "Go ahead. Make your phone call. Call whoever the hell you want. Your partner. Your mom. Your girlfriend."

At the word *girlfriend* Jon let out an involuntary sigh. The commander was right. Jon had to call Ali.

Not just had to, he *wanted* to call her. Wanted to

hear her voice after all he'd been through, but he knew it wasn't going to be that easy. She'd been in the dark for weeks, and she wasn't going to be happy about it.

No doubt she'd let him know that.

Fighting ISIS had probably been easier than facing Ali would be after this. He hoped he proved as capable in that upcoming battle as he had been in this last one.

"Thank you, sir. I appreciate it."

"Yeah, I guess I owe you one."

While he was asking for favors, Jon figured it wouldn't hurt to tack on one more. "I wouldn't mind a shower and to shave too. If it's possible."

The commander cocked a brow. "Tell the aide outside to drive you over to the other side of camp. There's a communications center and a shower building."

"Yes, sir. Thank you."

With the flick of a wrist, the commander dismissed both Jon and his thanks.

That was fine. Jon had calls to make. As he walked he decided he'd call Zane first and save Ali for last. Kind of work his way up in degree of difficulty.

Zane would be pissed too that Jon had kept this job secret from him, but he'd get over it quick enough. Ali, on the other hand . . .

He stopped at the aide's desk. "The commander said to ask you to drive me over to the communications center and the showers."

Slack mouthed, the kid raised his gaze from the computer. "He told me I need to get this done and on his desk in the next fifteen minutes or else."

"Just point me in the direction and I'll get there myself." Jon had made it from Virginia, to Turkey, to Mosul, to Camp Swift. He figured he could make it across camp on his own.

The man gave him quick directions and Jon was off. He was happy to be on his way. Less happy to be walking across an American camp looking too much like an ISIS fighter thanks to the beard, hair and black clothes. But he figured without a weapon he shouldn't be too much of a target for any trigger happy soldiers. At least that's what he hoped.

Jon had just made it out the door when he heard, "Hey, American!"

Turning, he saw a Peshmerga soldier across the yard, holding a weapon high in the air and grinning. Jon had a feeling the rifle was one of the pieces they'd recovered after the attack.

Smiling, he waved in return. He'd done the right thing by coming here. He would have to keep that in mind, because the hard part was yet to come.

A vehicle skidded to a stop next to him, kicking up dust and rocks into the air. "Need a ride?"

Jon turned at the familiar voice, shocked to see an old friend. "Gordo?"

Hanging out the open side of a small truck with the doors removed was a guy Jon had gone through BUD/S with.

His friend was a little older and a lot bulkier, as if he'd been pumping a whole lot of iron in his downtime. But there was no doubt it was him.

Gordo grinned. "In the flesh. I barely recognized you with that long ass beard you're sporting. What the fuck is Jon Rudnick doing in this hellhole? I heard you got out."

Jon laughed. "I did get out of the Navy but not out of the business. I'm here probably for the same reason you are."

The man tipped his head. "Well, there are only two things to do here in lovely Makhmour. Fight ISIS and try to keep the Iraqis and the Peshmerga from turning on each other, so it must be one of those."

Grinning, Jon said, "I'd put my money on the Kurds in that fight."

"Smart man. So you're working private military now." Gordo let out a loud belly laugh. "I bet the commander just loves you."

Jon nodded. "So you know him."

"Oh, yeah. And he makes no secret of how he feels about PMCs. So how long you here for?" Gordo asked.

"If the commander doesn't decide to throw me in the brig, I'm hoping they'll arrange transport as soon as possible."

Gordo laughed. "If he does lock you up we'll break you out. I got a team of frogmen with me who've got your six. No worries."

"Good to hear. Thanks. Is there anybody else I know here with you? Brody Cassidy and his team been through?"

"Nope. Just my unit from Team Three. That's it. POTUS is trying to keep this party small. So where you headed? Need a ride?"

"I need a shower and a shave and to call home."

"I think I can hook you up with all of that plus

some. Hop in."

"Thanks." Jon circled the truck and slid into the open passenger side. An old friend. A shower—hot or cold, he didn't care which at this point. A long overdue shave. Things were certainly looking up.

That things were going so good should have made Jon nervous. The surest way to tempt fate was to be happy. Jon reminded himself of that as he bounced in the passenger seat while Gordo sped through camp way too fast.

He barely slowed in front of a cluster of buildings before skidding to a hard stop, apparently not a fan of going light on the brakes.

"My humble abode is at your disposal—" An explosion that rocked the very air surrounding them cut off Gordo.

"What the fuck?" Jon leaned out the open doorway to try and see what was happening.

"RPG!" The shout came from a man running toward them. From the way he was dressed, Jon figured he was one of Gordo's team.

"Shit." Gordo turned to Jon, mouth open to say something that he never had a chance to as the concussion of another rocket-propelled grenade explosion hit close, shattering the windshield.

It lifted the light truck Jon and Gordo still sat in. Jon felt the force of the concussion from the blast throwing him backward in the seat as the vehicle upended.

Upside down, covered in glass, with dirt in his eyes blinding him and his hearing gone from the explosion, all Jon could think was he'd been so close to getting home. So close . . .

CHAPTER SEVENTEEN

In what had become her usual place and position of late, Ali sat on the sofa with the television playing softly as she tried not to get so stressed she needed to vomit.

There was one difference though . . . unlike the other night when Darci couldn't get in touch with her with news of Jon, Ali had her cell phone in view, fully charged and with the volume turned all the way up.

She shouldn't care if she did miss a call. Jon obviously didn't care about her. She'd had to get the message he was alive fourth-hand. Some military or government guy had apparently called Zane to confirm the identity of a man claiming to be Jon Rudnick. Zane had contacted Chris, who'd told Darci to call Ali.

That might be fifth-hand information, now that she thought about it.

Her anger returned, like it so often did—when she wasn't crying, that was.

Damn hormones.

Yet here she sat, waiting. Waiting and worrying. Upset, angry . . . helpless.

She waited so hard that the sound of the cell phone ringing startled her into a jump that knocked the remote control off her lap.

It was probably just Darci checking on her again.

Leaning over, Ali grabbed the cell off the coffee table and saw an unfamiliar number on the readout.

Would the military call her cell about Jon if something happened to him? They weren't married so would she be notified at all?

Feeling sick, she answered. "Hello?"

"Hi, it's me." Jon's voice cut through some static. He sounded distant but clear enough she recognized that it was him without doubt.

Yup, she heard every word.

Hi, it's me.

That's all he had to say to her after disappearing for weeks without a single word? And after her having to hear through what amounted to a telephone chain that he was alive somewhere. And her having to wonder all this time since then where, with whom and in what condition he was in.

"Hi." She somehow managed that single word. Her heart pounded with a mix of emotions that raged through her. Determined to get answers to at least some of her many questions, she asked, "Where are you?"

"Um . . ." As he paused, likely trying to decide which lie or half truth to tell her, Ali realized how stupid she'd been to ask.

Jon had never in all the years she'd known him, dated him, loved him, told her precisely where he was when he was working. When he had given her a location, she always suspected it was a lie. No man went on that many "trainings" in the middle of the desert where there was no internet or cell service, she didn't care if he had been an elite SEAL at the time.

Back peddling, she switched gears. "Can you at least tell me if you're okay?"

"Yeah. I'm fine." There was no hesitation before that answer.

It was Jon's favored response but Ali had long ago learned that the word *fine* was a relative term.

Rick had a bullet pass through his chest and said he was fine. Thom had gotten such a severe concussion he had temporary memory loss, but he went right back to his team because he too was fine.

Knowing that *fine* was the best she was going to get from him, Ali chose to accept the answer. He was good enough to speak to her. That would have to do to ease her mind.

"Can you tell me when you might be home?"

Although sometimes she'd forget, Ali had also learned to phrase her questions differently after being with Jon. To no longer ask things like *when* or *where*, but rather could he tell her?

"Not long, I hope."

Not long. Another non-answer. What exactly did that mean?

"So a couple of days? Weeks? Months?" Her voice cracked on the last word. Frustrated, she felt the hot tears prickling behind her eyes.

In a couple of months she'd be showing. At least that would solve the problem of how to tell him. Then she could just flash him her big rounded belly and say *surprise.*

"Probably days but—"

"I know. Don't hold you to that." Ali had already heard all the excuses for his delays. Weather. Transportation issues. Paperwork problems. She didn't need to hear them again.

"How are you doing?" Jon's question got her full attention.

Ali hadn't confided in anyone about the baby yet. Not even Darci. So far only she and the doctor knew. But Ali had told Darci she was late. And she also was there when Ali had fainted.

Had Darci told Chris that Ali could be pregnant? Chris could have easily told Jon. She hadn't wanted him to find out like that. Heck, she was torn if she wanted to tell him at all.

Of course, she would have to, but she really wasn't looking forward to seeing the look in his eyes. He'd feel responsible and trapped and do the one thing he hadn't been willing to do before the baby.

He'd marry her.

If she couldn't have him as her husband because he felt that she was the one person he couldn't live without, the one woman he wanted to grow old with, she didn't want him at all.

"Why? What did you hear?" Her suspicions

sounded loudly in her own ears.

"I haven't heard anything. I haven't spoken to anyone there. You're my first call."

God, how she wanted to believe him. For so many reasons.

"Not even Zane?" she asked.

"Nope. I am going to call him next though." He sounded sincere, and a little confused by her inquisition.

"Okay." She swallowed away the sick feeling and realized she'd never answered his question. "I'm fine."

There was a certain satisfaction in turning his words back on him. Let him wonder exactly what that answer meant, like she'd had to for years.

"Look, I hate to do this, but I have to cut this short."

"All right." She had plenty more to say but, as usual, she'd have to wait and do it on Jon's schedule.

"I love you." He said the three words so easily, even though his actions didn't always support them.

But Jon wasn't home yet and if she had to venture a guess, it would be that he probably wasn't out of danger yet either.

Ali resisted the urge to be petty and angry and said, "I love you too."

CHAPTER EIGHTEEN

One down, one more to go . . .

The call to Ali hadn't gone quite as badly as he'd expected. Then again, it had been short. He was sure she'd put a pin in her anger and this was going to be continued later.

That was fine. He'd be happy to be home and with her, yelling or not.

Next up, the partner he'd lied to. Jon checked the battery life on the cell phone he'd gotten from Gordo and quickly typed in a text message to Zane, asking him to call.

The cell lit up within seconds of him hitting send on the message. Jon hit the button to answer. "Hey."

"Where are you?" Zane cut right to the point without pausing for a greeting.

"At the moment? Germany."

"And where were you before Germany?"

"Iraq." Jon braced himself for his friend's reaction to his answer.

"Yeah. I kind of guessed that when I got a call from some lieutenant working for the commander at Camp Swift asking if I could verify you were actually you. All right, now you've confirmed it that brings me to my next question. What the fuck are you doing there?"

"I took a solo assignment."

The sound of Zane's snort came through Jon's cell. "Obviously. Wanna tell me whom you were working for?"

"That's classified." Jon cringed, knowing that answer wasn't going to be well received.

Zane paused before saying, "Okay. So that tells me it was for the government. My guess would be FBI, CIA, or DHS but I'll stop with the departmental alphabet soup and move on. What can you tell me? You took a job doing what?"

As much as it hurt his bruised body, Jon let out a laugh at Zane's accurate guesses. The man had worked in the shadows as long as Jon had. He knew the deal.

Jon trusted Zane but he could still only tell him part of the story without breaking operational security. "I was infiltrating a certain enemy organization who should probably vet their recruited foreign fighters a bit more carefully in future."

Even with his ears still ringing from the blast, Jon heard Zane's sigh. "And you chose not to tell me why?"

"I was undercover. You know the fewer people who know the better. It's safer for everyone, you included."

"I'm your fucking partner . . ." Zane blew out a loud breath. "You know what, we can talk about this when you get home. When will that be, approximately?"

"I'm hoping to get released today." Jon had realized his mistake even before Zane started cursing at him. He could only blame the slip on his injuries.

"*Released?* Motherfucker. You're in the hospital and you don't think to tell me that?"

"It's nothing."

"Oh, really? Okay then, give me a list of the nothings that have you in the hospital waiting to be released."

"Concussion. Light shrapnel wounds. Nothing I haven't had before. Like I told you. It's nothing."

"All that nothing adds up to tell me you were most likely on the wrong end of a blast. An IED. Or an RPG, maybe."

Jon let out a short laugh and felt the resulting ache. "You are just full of letters today."

"Yeah, well since you're more full of shrapnel than answers, I have to be."

"Nah, they got most of it out, I think." He'd been lucky. Gordo had been too. The vehicle had shielded them from the worst of the explosion.

Jon heard his doctor's voice just outside in the hallway. "Zane, I gotta go and see about getting out of here."

"Call me when you're stateside."

"I will."

"And you better call Ali, bro. I heard from Chris a couple of days ago that she's not too happy."

"Already called her, but thanks for the concern. I'll talk to you later." Jon happily disconnected before Zane tried to give him any more relationship advice.

God, how Jon hated everyone being in his business, even if they were friends. It was his own fault. He'd left Ali. Of course she'd turn to their friends for support in his absence. But he'd be home soon and straighten everything out.

At least Jon hoped he'd be home soon.

As the doctor came through the doorway, he figured he'd know one way or another soon enough.

CHAPTER NINETEEN

Just as the commander at Camp Swift had been anxious to get rid of Jon and had shipped him immediately off to the military hospital in Germany, the powers that be there had also made sure to get Jon out of the country and out of their hair as soon as the doctor released him and transport was logistically feasible. Even if a couple of the legs of his journey were less than safe, he was finally home.

As he felt the Virginia air on his face, he realized they could have asked him to walk through fire and if it meant being here—home—he would have willingly and gladly done it.

His euphoria lasted the whole cab ride from the airport to the office, where he picked up his keys and his truck. Jon didn't even care that it had started to rain during the short drive from the office to his house. The closer he got to home, the more real it felt.

Real and surreal and wonderful all at the same time.

Jon drove faster than he should have given the conditions and it wasn't long before he stood at the door of his condo.

He drew in a big breath as the emotions he'd kept on lockdown while he'd been gone started to surface, unlocked the door and swung it open.

The first sight to greet him was Ali, curled up on the sofa, wrapped in a blanket.

At the sound of his entering, she spun around. Her eyes flew wide when she saw him in the doorway . . . before they narrowed beneath her frown.

"Nice to see you made it home alive. And nice to see that you finally shaved." She'd obviously gotten over her shock of seeing him home and had moved right on to her anger over him being gone.

It didn't take a genius to see she was good and pissed at him, but he didn't care. He'd been to hell, danced with the devil and made it back to her and he'd be damned if he wasn't going to at least kiss her now.

Determined, he strode across the room, pulled her off the sofa and drew her to him in an embrace that was as much for his benefit as hers.

She let him hold her, but she remained stiff in his arms. He decided to take what he could get and be grateful.

"I know you're mad but it's so good to hold

you." The words were muffled as he clasped her tight and buried his face against her hair. She smelled familiar and felt like home.

He'd missed her. He didn't realize how much until now while she was in his arms. He pulled back and tipped her face up. There was no controlling the urge to take her mouth.

The danger of posing as an ISIS fighter hadn't scared him as much as knowing that just days away from being safely home and with Ali he'd nearly died.

It only proved what he knew already. No one could predict what could happen or when. He could live to a hundred or he could die tomorrow. It was about time he started really living.

"God, I missed you." The words were barely out before he crushed his mouth against hers.

Overwhelmed by the need to feel safe and alive, he kissed her hard and thoroughly. The long list of miracles that had brought him home mostly unscathed grew by one more when Ali didn't push him away.

She sank into his kiss, clinging to him through the jacket he'd never taken the time to remove.

He wanted to get her to the bedroom. Wanted the clothes separating them—his damp ones and her warm ones—gone.

But he wanted something else more.

Breaking the kiss, he blurted out the words that would make her his for the rest of his life. "Marry me."

She pulled back from him. "What?"

"Marry me." Now that he'd said it once, the

words spilled out even easier.

Her eyes narrowed. "Why are you asking me that now?"

"What?" He was too confused to comprehend her frown or the suspicion in her tone. Wasn't this what she'd wanted?

"Did you come right here or stop somewhere first?"

Further confused by that question, he said, "I stopped at the office."

Her nostrils flared. She was mad he went to the office?

He continued, trying to diffuse this bomb while blind. "I had to. My truck was parked in the lot. And my house keys were there too. Ali, I don't know what's happening here. All I know is I want to marry you."

"You didn't before you left."

"I did. I just—"

"I can't be here with you right now." After cutting him off she moved toward the door.

What the fuck had just happened?

How could things have gone to shit so fast? All he'd done was try to give her what she wanted. What he now realized he wanted too.

He knew one thing, as the tears streamed down her face and she struggled to get her shoes on by the door, he wasn't going to be able to reason with her now.

"Ali. You stay. I'll go." Confused at why she refused to be under the same roof as him, Jon still wasn't going to make her go out in the rain just to get away from him.

He knew he could crash at Chris and Brody's apartment for the night. The office was probably a better bet. He really didn't want to deal with any questions. This was his mess and he'd deal with it on his own in private.

"No. You stay. This is your place. It was never mine. I can sleep at Darci's. She already offered me Rick's bedroom."

Why the hell would Darci be offering her a place to sleep when Ali was living with him? What had happened while he'd been gone? Had Ali been confiding in Darci about wanting to leave him?

He had a feeling he wouldn't like the answer.

Meanwhile, Ali continued to ramble as she reached for her jacket. "Sierra's in LA filming a movie and Rick will be out there with her for the next few weeks. It's been all over the television . . . but you wouldn't know that since you haven't been around."

He didn't argue that he probably wouldn't have known about Sierra and her movie even if he had been around. If Rick wasn't Darci's brother, and Darci wasn't Ali's best friend, Sierra Cox wouldn't even be on Jon's radar.

He honestly couldn't give a shit where Rick was at the moment. All he could focus on was that she was leaving for some reason he couldn't even begin to guess. "Ali, I don't want you to go. Can't we talk about this?"

Dry-eyed now, she just shook her head. "I'm not sure you know what you want, Jon."

There was no anger in the statement. Just resignation.

Jon would rather she yell at him. Rant. Throw things.

At least that would show some passion and make him feel as if she cared. Not like this new freakish calm that had settled over her as she grabbed her purse and walked out the door and out of his life.

CHAPTER TWENTY

It was getting too late for any respectable person to just show up unannounced, even at a friend's house. That didn't stop Ali as she arrived at Darci's place and swung the car into her drive.

It had been all Ali could do to hold on to the steering wheel and see the road. With the rain on the windshield and her hot tears making it even harder to see, she didn't have it in her to multitask and make a call.

Given these were extenuating circumstances she didn't give the lateness of the hour more than a passing thought as she rang the bell. She did however notice her hands trembling as she did.

With a sense of urgency riding her, just pushing the tiny button wasn't enough to ease her agitation. She moved on to pounding on Darci's door.

It swung open beneath her raised fist.

Chris stood in the doorway, all six foot plus of him looking concerned as he reached for her arms and looked her up and down before his gaze swept the driveway and road. "Ali, what's wrong? Are you a'ight?"

He wouldn't find the reason for her distress out there—unless of course Jon had followed her.

Ali resisted the urge to look and instead asked, "Where's Darci?"

"I'm right here. What's happening?" Darci peered past her fiancé. "Chris, let her in. It's raining."

As a testament to the fact she wasn't in her right mind at the moment, Ali hadn't noticed that the persistent drizzle had soaked her hair until she got inside and a drop of water trickled down her forehead.

"Come sit down. Chris, get a towel." Darci led Ali to the sofa.

He moved to the kitchen and pulled a dishtowel out of a drawer, only to pause as he pressed his cell to his ear. "Hey. Yeah, she's here."

The words, softly spoken as he glanced at Ali in the living room set off her warning bells.

"Who is that?" Ali glared at Chris, suspecting she already knew the answer.

He held up one hand to silence her, which only made her angry. Darci covered Ali's hand with hers and silently watched Chris's one-sided conversation along with her.

"Okay. Will do. Talk to you later." Chris disconnected the call and came to where they sat.

He handed the towel to Ali. "Jon just wanted to make sure you made it here safe and sound since you were upset when you left."

"He's home? That's great." Darci squeezed Ali's hand before releasing her hold.

"You'd think so, wouldn't you?" Ali let out a snort and patted her face and hair with the towel. She looked back to Chris. "What else did he say?"

"That if you need anything, just call."

"That's it?" she asked, suspicious.

"That's it, Ali. I swear." Chris held up his hand to make that pledge.

She believed him. This kind of behavior was typical Jon. Thoughtful and caring, but only when it didn't matter.

He'd gladly drive over in the rain to deliver her clothes and a toothbrush, but when it came to the important stuff—such as telling her when he was leaving the country for a month for some deadly assignment—*that* he neglected to do.

She had run out of the house with nothing but the clothes on her back and the junk in her purse, but she'd rather go to bed in her underwear and without brushing her teeth than ask Jon to bring her anything.

Darci would have things she could borrow and tomorrow she could sneak home and get her stuff from the condo. No doubt Jon would be out of the house and at the office bright and early, as usual. His workaholic habits made him predictable and she was going to use that to her advantage.

"Now that *that* is settled, what happened?" Darci asked.

Ali drew in a breath and blurted, "He asked me to marry him."

Darci's eyes flew wide. "What? That's amazing."

"No, it's not."

"When did he get home?" Chris asked.

"About two minutes before he proposed." Ali turned to Darci. "See the problem?"

"No." Darci shook her head. "Maybe he just finally came to his senses while he was away."

Ali glanced at Chris and saw his lips pressed tightly into a thin line, as if he was physically holding in his commentary on the matter. She decided to get it out of him. "Chris?"

Darci swung her gaze to her fiancé. "What do you think?"

After a pause where he looked like he was wrestling with the decision to say anything, he finally drew in a breath. "I think you and Jon should just sit tight, wait a little while and then revisit this marriage discussion."

That all sounded very logical, except Ali didn't believe that was all. Chris's strained expression was confirmation of her suspicion.

"And?" she asked.

He closed his eyes before opening them and focusing on her. "From what I heard from Zane, it sounds like Jon was in the middle of some serious shit . . . This could be in reaction to that."

"See!" Ali spun to Darci.

"Hang on there. I'm not saying he'll change his mind but—"

"It's probably some knee jerk reaction to almost

getting himself killed," Ali cut in to finish Chris's sentence.

Almost killed.

The words hit her hard as she realized he really could have almost died. Judging by the cuts she'd seen on his face, something bad had happened.

She pressed her hand to her stomach as it tossed with more than just pregnancy hormones.

"So? Do what Chris says. Let the discussion ride for a bit then you'll see that he does want to marry you. I'm sure he always did, he was just too busy with GAPS."

And that hadn't changed. The company hadn't gone away. It was still there—Jon's mistress.

But something had changed. Jon wouldn't be committing to a future with just Ali any longer. There was a baby he knew nothing about.

"There's more." Ali raised her gaze. "I'm pregnant."

Her friend sucked in a breath. "Oh my God!"

"Darci, stop. I did not tell you so we can celebrate. I'm telling you because I need to know if either of you told Jon anything. Gave him any hint at all about my telling you last week that I was late."

Darci shook her head. "I didn't say anything, Ali."

"Swear to me."

"I swear. How and when would I have talked to Jon?" Darci asked.

"Maybe you didn't but Chris might have. Or Zane could have."

Looking a little pale, Chris shook his head. "Uh,

yeah. No. First off, I didn't know anything about your um . . . cycle, so there was no way I could have told Zane or Jon anything. And I promise you I haven't talked to Jon. I didn't even know he was back."

"It doesn't matter if Jon knows about the baby or not. He didn't want to be with me before he left. And he only thinks he wants to be with me now because he probably almost died. But I know him and he'll do the honorable thing and force himself to marry me because I'm pregnant and it's the right thing to do."

"But Jon did want to be with you. He asked you to move in with him. That's a huge step. It's like being married, but without the paperwork."

Ali scowled at Darci's reasoning. "He asked me because my lease was up, my rent was going to skyrocket, and it was most practical for me to move in."

Jon was nothing if not thrifty and practical.

"No." Darci shook her head. "That all might have been a factor in the timing but he asked you to move in because he loves you."

"Oh, he loves me. But still look what he does to me. He disappears. If he doesn't outright lie, he at the very least avoids telling me the truth."

"That's his life." Again, Darci took Jon's side. It was starting to piss Ali off. Darci was supposed to be her friend.

"No, it *was* his life in the SEALs. He's no longer in the SEALs, is he?"

Sighing as Ali's argument took the wind out of her sails, Darci glanced up at Chris. "Ali does have a good point. You work for GAPS and yes there are certain details you won't tell me but I never feel like Ali does. That you are consistently withholding the truth."

Chris lifted a shoulder. "It's not my company. I'm only privy to what pertains to me and my specific assignment. Jon's the keeper of all the information, some of it top secret. It makes sense he'd be cautious. The company's reputation depends on it."

Ali let out a huff. "Then he can just marry the company."

Chris drew in a breath and let it out, silently giving up the fight with her. Probably because with that last statement she sounded like a child and only a fool would argue with a child. Chris Cassidy was no fool.

Given that, Ali should probably listen to him.

Maybe tomorrow.

CHAPTER TWENTY-ONE

It had been a long night for Jon alone in the bed where Ali should have been with him. If he hadn't been exhausted from traveling he probably wouldn't have slept at all. As it was, he got a restless sleep and woke up not long after dawn.

Rather than hang out at the condo reliving the shit storm of the night before, he made coffee and headed right out for the office. At least there he'd be busy. All the work that had no doubt accumulated while he was gone and a full email inbox would keep his mind occupied until Ali decided to talk to him again.

Jon opened the office door and found Chris was already there. The man glanced up from the coffee maker when Jon walked in.

"Hey, bubba. Good to see you back in one

piece." Chris's tone was ripe with unspoken questions and comments.

"Thanks." Jon could only imagine what Chris knew and what he was thinking given that Ali had gone directly to Darci's last night. He decided to redirect the conversation away from his personal life. "By the way, I didn't see Brody or any of his team where I was."

"And where was that exactly?" Chris cocked up one brow.

With a sigh, Jon decided he might as well spill. The op was over and since his picture would be plastered all over for every ISIS fighter, leader and recruiter to see, he wouldn't be going back. At least not in the same capacity as last time.

"Makhmour."

Chris nodded. "A'ight. Thanks. That narrows down my choices of where he might be. If they weren't in Makhmour with you, Brody could be part of that big push to retake Fallujah."

Jon cringed. "That's where Mack was with his old unit when Speedy was killed. That fucked up Mack's head pretty bad for a while. It's why he got himself transferred to Brody's team and now he could be right back where he started."

"Yup. Let's hope for everyone's sake it's been long enough now he's channeled all that emotional shit and can focus on the mission."

Jon hoped so too. From what little he knew of the man, Mack could be intense sometimes.

But SEAL team dynamics weren't Jon's problem anymore and hadn't been since he'd left the Navy and formed GAPS. The pissed off look on his partner's face as Zane walked in the front door though—that definitely was Jon's problem.

Zane directed a glare at Jon. "Let's go in the back room."

After their talk on the phone from his hospital bed, Jon had thought he might get away without a lecture from Zane. Apparently he'd been wrong.

Bracing himself for the worst, Jon followed Zane to the meeting room. He sat. Zane didn't, which didn't bode well.

"What you did goes against all of our training. One man on his own is not a militarily significant unit." Zane launched right into the lecture.

"I know."

Jon was very aware that there was always a *lost man plan* for every op, but he didn't unconditionally believe the military's philosophy that a single man was nothing without a group backing him up. Sometimes one could move more easily—accomplish greater things—than six or even two.

Shaking his head, Zane continued, "You say you know, but yet you go and pull a Bergdahl? You know better than that shit, Jon."

Bowe Bergdahl, the soldier who wanted to be a lone hero and see some action. The act of him leaving his base and going off on his own, only to be captured by the enemy, cost him years of his life and the military thousands of dollars. Not to mention he put his fellow troops at risk as they attempted to get him back.

Bergdahl had been ridiculously foolish, and Zane was calling Jon stupid with the comparison. But Zane lobbing insults didn't change anything.

That didn't stop the man from continuing his rant. "And you know what? I should have seen this coming. The minute Chris told me you'd been growing your beard and not cutting your hair I should have known you were preparing to take on ISIS. But dammit, Jon, I never thought I'd have to play mommy to my own partner. Did you not see that ISIS is killing their own people looking for spies? Hell of a time to go over there as an actual damn spy!"

Zane's nostrils flared and he drew in a breath after that tirade. Jon hoped he was done, but he was wrong.

"And what about Ali? Do you realize how worried she was?"

"I know." Jon didn't need Zane to remind him that if he couldn't make things right with her this mission—whether justified or not—could cost him Ali.

Chris, who'd been leaning against the doorframe in the open doorway silently observing Zane's rant until now, finally joined the conversation. He pushed off the wall and took a step into the room. "I'm not sure you do know how bad it was for her."

Jon sighed. Now Chris was against him too. "I told her not to worry before I left."

"You *told her not to worry*? Are you fucking kidding me? Do you not know women at all?" Zane threw his hands in the air, as if he was done with the whole mess and Jon.

If only that were true. Unfortunately Jon had a feeling this was far from done.

Chris shook his head. "Buddy, it was bad here. Hell, if last night was any indication, it still is bad. And being engaged to Darci, I get a front row seat to the whole clusterfuck. Jon, the day we got word from Zane you'd been found and we went to tell Ali, she collapsed. Like literally went down. I grabbed her before she hit her head and we stayed with her all night but still . . ."

Jon bit out a curse and then raised his eyes to Chris. "Thank you for being there for her."

Chris raised a brow. "Of course, I'd be there for her. That ain't the point. You have some work to do. Make that a *lot* of work to do repairing your relationship. And I suggest you do it ASAP."

"I know." It seemed he'd been saying that a lot today. But knowing he'd screwed things up and knowing what to do to fix it were two very different things. "Unfortunately, she's not exactly talking to me right now. She won't respond to my texts. Won't answer my calls. Hard to apologize when she won't listen."

Chris widened his eyes. "Then make her listen."

Not sure why Chris was so invested in his relationship with Ali, Jon said, "Okay. I'll try."

"Maybe send her some flowers. Or chocolate. Little things like that can go a long way to getting a girl over her mad," Chris suggested.

"Diamonds go even further." Zane, born and raised by parents so rich Jon couldn't even guess their net worth, added his two cents.

Even if he could afford the kind of gifts Zane was talking about, Jon knew Ali. He wasn't sure diamonds would do any good. "At this point, I have a feeling she'd throw anything I gave her back in my face."

"That's why I always have my make-up gifts delivered. Softens her up first before I show my face." Zane grinned, making Jon laugh in spite of his misery.

Chris shook his head. "Don't listen to Casanova here. You need to romance her. I bet that's what she's been missing now that you're living together and with you working so much. The romance."

Jon took his words into consideration. Chris could be right. "All right. I'll think about it."

Chris, who was probably more than tired of being caught in the middle of this mess, cocked a brow. "Think fast."

Just like in a mission, sometimes taking action was the only way to get out of the shit and Jon was certainly in the shit right now. But he'd get himself out of it. Somehow.

After the wake up call in Iraq, he might actually be motivated enough to get his work-life balance in order.

If he'd learned anything through all this mess, it was that there was more to living than the job. And love was a huge part of life.

Romance . . . Hell, why not? He could do romance. It might even be fun. He just hoped it would win him Ali back.

CHAPTER TWENTY-TWO

Ali had forced herself to go to work even though she had barely slept. She didn't even want to get out of bed, forget about put on clothes and interact with people. But she figured she'd better start banking her time off.

Given her current situation, there'd be doctor appointments and who knew what else she might need time off for. What kind of maternity leave did the bank give employees anyway? She'd never had reason to ask. She sure did now.

That frightening reality had been in her mind day and night since the doctor had delivered the news. Ali had a feeling that wasn't going to change.

"Ali?"

She glanced across the car at Darci. "Yeah?"

"You coming inside?" Darci had the driver's side

door partially open and her seatbelt off as she frowned at Ali, still buckled in the passenger seat.

They were in Darci's driveway and she hadn't even noticed.

Yup, it had definitely been for the best that they had carpooled to work today in Darci's car. Ali was obviously way too distracted to navigate rush hour traffic.

"Yeah." Blowing out a breath, she disconnected the seatbelt and swung her door open, only to realize she'd never gone over to the condo to get any of her stuff.

She'd been lucky that she had two work outfits in her car that she'd picked up from the dry cleaners. With the distraction of finding out she was pregnant, she forgotten about the dry cleaning bag in the backseat.

Luckily, she and Darci wore the same size shoe.

Those were the only reasons Ali had something besides her yoga pants and sneakers to wear to work.

Darci was the perfect host. She'd given Ali a brand new toothbrush and had shared her toiletries and makeup, but eventually she needed her own stuff.

And if she really did decide she couldn't stay with Jon, she'd have to find someplace to live as well.

"You doing okay?" Darci asked as she unlocked the front door of the house.

"Just thinking how I can't live with you forever."

"You could if you want to."

Ali laughed. "Yeah, I'm sure Chris would love that. You two being newlyweds and me hanging around."

"We haven't even set a date yet."

"You will though. And then there's Rick—"

"Rick has a rich girlfriend he can stay with. You're fine in his room. Don't worry about that. My name is on this house, not my brother's."

"Thank you, but still, I have to do something eventually."

"You could talk to Jon," Darci suggested, pausing in her path toward the kitchen.

Ali followed her friend, hoping she was going to make some tea. "I could."

"But?"

Ali opened her mouth to say she wasn't ready to talk to Jon yet, when a box on the counter caught her eye. "What's that?"

"I don't know." Darci walked closer and then smiled. "But it says *Ali* on the card."

"It does?" She frowned and moved to stand next to Darci. The box did indeed have an envelope with her name on it, written in Jon's handwriting.

"Aren't you going to open it?" Darci asked.

"Okay." Suddenly shaking, Ali reached for the envelope. After pulling out the card, she flipped it open and read the contents aloud for Darci's benefit. "*I know you've been wanting one.*"

"One of what?" Darci asked.

Ali looked at the box. "Good question."

There was only one way to find out. She tore at the wrapping paper and saw the printed box. "It's a

VCR."

"A what?" Darci laughed. "Do they still make those? And why in the world did you want one? Don't you have a DVD player?"

"Yes, but I have all of my favorite Christmas movies on tape. Last year my VCR broke. I figured if I couldn't find a new player to buy I'd have to replace all the movies with DVDs." Tears clouded Ali's eyes. "I didn't realize Jon even knew how upset I was about it."

"I guess he did."

Darci was right. Amazingly Jon had known and remembered and he'd somehow found a player to buy for her.

"What are you going to do? Are you going to text him? Or call so he knows you got it?" Darci asked.

Ali glanced up to find Darci watching her. The gift had been left in the house with her name on it, so Jon shouldn't doubt that she'd gotten it. Darci was obviously playing peacemaker by trying to get Ali to call Jon.

"I'm going to get changed out of my work clothes. That's what I'm going to do." Abandoning the box with Darci, Ali headed for the bedroom.

She was barely through the bedroom door when she saw her suitcase on the bed with yet another note. Not sure if she was ready for more assaults on her emotions, she reached for the folded paper.

Ali, I thought you might need a few things. I'd rather have you come home but if you need some time away I understand. I love you. Yours always,

Jon

With her heart twisted tight, Ali opened the bag.

One glance inside showed her he'd packed everything she would have grabbed herself. Hairbrush, toothbrush and a bag of toiletries and makeup. One of her favorite work outfits including the heels she always wore with it. Underwear, a bra and even her comfy old pajamas and fuzzy socks.

And, as detail oriented as ever, he'd put in her cell phone charger.

The choice of clothes, the attention to what she loved best, proved Jon was more observant than she'd given him credit for.

"You okay?" Darci's voice behind her had Ali turning.

There were tears in her eyes when she nodded. "Yeah. He, uh, dropped off a bag of my stuff."

Darci frowned. "So what does that mean? I refuse to believe he's fine with you moving out. Is he just going to give up on you two?"

Ali glanced from the note on the bed to the warm, worn PJs she'd snuggled in during so many nights. "No, I don't think he's giving up."

Typical Jon, he was laying a foundation to get her back. And if his intention was to slowly melt her frozen heart, it was working. She'd never been happier for Jon's single minded, goal oriented stubbornness than she was at this very moment.

"Your cell phone beeped." Darci walked in the room a bit farther. She handed Ali her purse, which contained her cell.

Ali had a feeling whom the text was from before

she dug out the cell and opened up the text. One glance confirmed it.

Let me know if you need anything else. I love you.

Ali felt the weight of Darci's scrutiny. She had to say something. "Um, I guess I should thank him."

Darci couldn't have beamed with a wider smile. "Good idea. We're out of lettuce so I'm running to the store. And you know, if you wanted to invite Jon over for dinner—"

Ali rolled her eyes. "Don't push it."

"I'm just saying. Dinner with the four of us might be a good way to break the ice between you two. They'll be no pressure since you won't be alone."

Ali pulled her mouth to one side. "I'll think about it."

"Okay." With another wide grin, Darci practically bounced out of the bedroom.

CHAPTER TWENTY-THREE

"Thanks for coming with me, Chris."

"No problem." Chris leaned against the display case and let out a long whistle. "Wow. I see you're following Zane's advice about the diamonds."

Jon smiled. "Not really. I shouldn't have proposed without a ring the first time."

He wouldn't make that mistake again. Maybe Ali would have reacted differently if he'd shown he'd been thinking about this for a while and it wasn't a knee jerk reaction to events in Iraq.

It wasn't that at all. Yeah, being on the wrong end of an RPG tends to make a man feel his mortality, but he always knew he wanted to marry Ali. He just moved on a slower timeline than some of the other guys. Such as Rocky, for instance.

The damn SEAL had proposed to a girl he barely

knew and Ali and Darci both thought it was the most romantic thing ever.

Crazy.

Ali moving in had been step one. His finishing this undercover job had been step two. He had wanted to wait for a holiday to make his proposal extra special—like the fourth of July when they'd first met, or New Year's Eve when he'd come home from deployment and they'd started dating—but that RPG was a wake up call.

Why should he wait when it was what they both wanted?

At least he'd thought it was what Ali wanted.

What the fuck had happened to change her mind? It couldn't be just that he'd sprung it on her. Surprise shouldn't send a woman running for the hills in hysterics.

He glanced at Chris. "Do you know of any other reason for her to react like this?"

Chris's eyes flew wide. "Me? Why would I know anything?"

"Maybe because you're engaged to—and practically living with—her best friend. And now she's staying there too."

Chris swung his head. "Nope. Don't know nothing."

"All right." Jon sighed. "Christ, some of these things are expensive."

He squinted at the tiny price tags in the case and wondered if the store had a liberal return policy just in case she said no.

"Why do you think I drove all the way to

Alabama? My grandma's ring was the right price for my taste. Free." Chris laughed. "And Darci got all choked up because it was from my family."

"Yeah, you lucked out having an heirloom. I've got nothing like that in my family." As Jon continued to peruse the choices, Chris pulled out his cell phone.

"I just got a text from Darci. She wants me to invite you to dinner tonight."

Jon glanced up, afraid to get excited that this was the beginning of Ali's forgiving him. But he had left the gift and a suitcase for her. "Darci wants me over? Or Ali?"

"Don't know. I can ask." Chris held the phone in his hand, waiting for Jon's answer.

He shook his head. "I'm not coming unless the invitation is from Ali."

Ali couldn't be pushed. She needed to do things in her own time. He knew that after all these years. In that way, they were very similar.

"A'ight. I'll tell her." Chris punched in a text and waited.

Jon waited right along with him, his pulse speeding when he heard the alert for a reply.

Chris read the screen and then shook his head. "Sorry, dude."

He held up the cell for Jon to see.

I'm working on it. Fingers crossed.

Deflated, Jon tipped his head in a nod. "Okay. Thanks for asking."

He should be happy he had Darci in his corner for this fight. He'd be happier to not be having a fight at all.

Jon glanced up as the salesman finally finished with another customer and approached. "Can I help you?"

"Yeah." On to his plan. Jon drew in a deep breath. "I need to see some engagement rings."

~ * ~

"Can I help you with dinner?" Ali asked Darci.

"I'm good. Just going to throw together a quick salad. The lasagna is already in the oven. Oh, and I picked up some fresh bread while I was at the store."

"Great." Ali did her best to keep the sarcasm out of her tone since she was a guest.

Fresh bread, particularly if it was heated in the oven for just a bit to make the outside crusty and the inside warm enough to melt a pat of butter, was Ali's weakness. She wasn't going to be able to resist having a piece even if she really tried to avoid eating too many carbs.

To hell with it.

She wasn't going to be able to avoid gaining weight for the next seven months anyway. She might as well take advantage of it and enjoy a damn piece of bread.

While shaking the water off the wet lettuce she'd rinsed in the sink, Darci glanced at Ali.

"You can set the table if you want. Three places . . . unless you invited Jon. Then set four." The eternal matchmaker lobbed that not so subtle hint as Ali reached for the plates in the cabinet.

Ali didn't want to encourage Darci with an

answer, but it would be rude to not tell her hostess how many people she would be serving for dinner. "There's only three for dinner."

"Did you thank him for the VCR and for dropping off your clothes?"

"Not yet."

"You're going to though, right?" Darci interrogated Ali from behind the salad spinner.

Ali rolled her eyes at her meddling friend. "Yes, I will."

"When?"

Jeez. Apparently Darci wasn't going to let this go. "Right now."

Ali disconnected her cell phone from the charger and punched in a quick text. Maybe this was better, her not having time to think too much about it. Not agonizing over every word. Just a quick thanks and done. Perfect.

She hit send on the one line text and plugged the phone back in.

"What did you say?"

"Thanks for dropping that stuff off."

"That's it? Just like that?"

"Yes." There was nothing else to say as far as Ali was concerned.

But apparently there was more, because the phone beeped almost immediately after she'd set it down. She stared at it from a distance, like it was a snake about to strike.

Darci's eyes flew wide. "Oh my God. He's replying."

"Of course, he is. Probably just saying you're

welcome."

Jon was nothing if not polite—when he wasn't sneaking off to dangerous assignments without telling her.

She drew in a breath, grabbed the cell again and read the text aloud to her nosy friend, "*You're welcome*. See? I told you."

"Oh." Darci looked so disappointed, Ali laughed.

Feeling bad for not appreciating that all Darci wanted to do was help, Ali asked, "Want me to open a bottle of wine for you?"

Darci's pout deepened. "No. You can't have any."

Ali lifted one shoulder. "So? You still can. I'm pouring you a glass."

"Really, I don't need any wine."

"Darci, stop. I know you and there is no way I'm letting you have Italian food without a glass of red wine to go with it on my account." Ali was about to move toward the wine rack when her cell beeped again.

Darci whipped toward her, eyes wide. "Is it him?"

Suspecting that herself Ali reached for the phone one more time.

Can we talk in person? Somewhere alone. Not in front of Darci and Chris?

"Well?" Darci came closer so only the narrow width of the kitchen island separated them.

Ali put the phone face down on the end of the countertop out of Darci's reach. "He just says if I need anything else from home to let him know."

"Oh." Darci pursed her lips. "You could ask for something and then he'd have to come over to—"

"No." Ali cut that scheme off with a single firmly delivered word.

"Fine. I think I will open that wine." As Darci turned and headed for the dining room, Ali picked up the cell.

She punched in a single word.

Okay.

Pulse racing, she really wished she could have a drink.

CHAPTER TWENTY-FOUR

A soft beep from her cell on the nightstand had Ali rolling over. In the dark bedroom, the glow of the phone's display lit the whole side of the room with a blue light.

Are you awake?

She hadn't been asleep, not for lack of trying. But Jon's text message had her really awake now.

Yes.

She sent the reply and got a quick response.

Check outside the front door.

It was late, after eleven, but there was no question she was going to do exactly as the text instructed.

Heart pounding, she padded barefoot from the bedroom, down the hall and across the living room to the front door. Flipping the locks, she opened the door as quietly as possible so she wouldn't wake Darci and Chris.

Sitting on the top step outside was a vase overflowing with pink peonies.

More than the fact he'd remembered her favorite flower and hadn't gone with the typical choice of roses, she was pretty sure peonies weren't in season now. Jon would have had to search to find a florist with them in stock.

This man wasn't making it easy for her to stay mad at him.

Fine, she wasn't mad anymore, but that didn't change the fact there was now a baby on board Jon knew nothing about. And that would change everything.

She stood frozen, realizing he had to be close. Ali peered into the darkness, searching.

"Jon?" Her loud whisper didn't travel very far.

It turned out that it didn't have to. Jon stepped out from behind the shrub to the right of the doorway. "Hi."

The sight of him creeping out of the bushes and looking so contrite had her letting out a breathy laugh even as she got teary eyed.

Damn these pregnancy hormones.

She managed to not cry as she said, "Hi."

"Sorry. I wasn't planning on bothering you tonight. I just wanted to see if you found the flowers."

"You're not bothering me. And they're beautiful. Thank you."

He bent at the waist and picked up the

overflowing vase. Taking the final step up, he stood level with Ali in the doorway.

Jon held out the arrangement. "You're welcome. I'm glad you like them."

She more than liked them. She loved them. And him. So much.

The first tear spilled over the rim of her lower lid as she reached blindly for the vase.

Dammit.

With the flowers occupying both her hands she couldn't wipe the moisture away before he saw it.

"Ah, Ali." Without a moment's hesitation, he wrapped his arms around her.

She drew in a stuttering breath and leaned her forehead against the wall of his chest, the flowers getting crushed between them.

He sighed and dropped a kiss to the top of her head. They stood there in silence in the dark cold night for what seemed like a long while.

Jon didn't speak again, so she did. "Do you want to come inside?"

He nodded. "Yeah, I do."

Ali moved back and turned to lead the way. He closed the door softly behind him and followed her into the living room.

She stood, looking around and deciding where to put the flowers. For the time being, she set them on the kitchen island. But later—after Jon left and she went back to bed—she was bringing them to her room. Call her selfish, but she didn't feel like sharing.

"So, you said you wanted to talk?" she asked,

when she'd moved back to the living room.

"It's late. We don't have to—"

"No, it's okay. I was awake. I haven't been sleeping so great." She perched on the edge of the sofa, choosing that over a chair so he could sit there too.

"Yeah, I can understand that." He drew in a breath and sat next to her.

With the room illuminated by the overhead recessed lighting she'd flipped on to navigate her way to the door, she could see Jon clearly.

She hadn't noticed the full extent of his injuries at the condo. There was a dark bruise punctuated by a deep cut that had started to scab on his cheekbone.

When she looked closer she saw more similar injuries. "What—" She caught herself asking a question he probably wouldn't answer anyway and changed direction. "Are you okay?"

"Yeah." He reached out and took her hands in his. "Do you want to know what happened?"

Shocked at the offer, she quickly agreed. "Yes. Of course."

"I was in a truck that overturned."

She drew in a sharp breath. "Oh my God."

"It's okay. Just some cuts and bruises. A little bit of a concussion." He locked his gaze on hers. "One of the reasons I try not to tell you too many details is because knowing them would make it harder for you than not knowing. Like this time. What happened sounds a lot worse than the result because I really am fine."

She shook her head. "No, Jon. Trust me. Not

knowing is so much worse. That leaves room for my imagination to run wild. What I'm picturing is probably worse than reality."

"You do have an active imagination." His mouth quirked up in the corner. "Okay. I'll try to communicate better. Tell you what I can. When I can."

"And I'll try not to get mad when there are things you can't tell me."

"Thank you." He let out a soft laugh. "Hey, look. This talking stuff actually works."

The joke from her ever-serious Jon twisted her heart. She forced a smile. "Yeah. Imagine that."

He was trying so hard. If a man were capable of changing, she knew that Jon, with his usual determination to excel at all things, would achieve it.

But his seeming openness to communicate and compromise didn't alter the reality the baby she carried would completely change his life, whether he was ready or not.

Wanting change was one thing. Having it forced on him was quite another. She couldn't stand to see resentment in his eyes when he looked at her, any more than she could stand living without him.

"I missed you." Jon shook his head. "No, present tense. I *miss* you."

"I miss you too." Squeezing his hands with hers, she moved closer to him on the sofa until their knees touched.

He leaned in and pressed his forehead against hers. "If you don't feel at home in the condo, we can move somewhere that feels like ours instead of just mine."

She pulled back to see him better. "You'd move for me?"

"Ali, yes. Of course. I'd kill or die for you. Moving is nothing."

Jon, when he was like this, made it so easy to see the light of hope for their future. Made the hell of the worry she'd endured seem distant.

The overwhelming shadow of the secret she kept from him seemed to recede a bit as Jon leaned down and hesitated just shy of her lips, watching her. Waiting.

She cupped his face with both hands and crashed her mouth against his.

Kissing Jon was comfortable. Familiar. She desperately needed to feel that right now.

It might be just avoidance on her part. Putting off the things she didn't want to think about, talk about, but she didn't care.

She could only be strong for so long. She needed a break. Needed to lean on Jon's strength for a bit. That need turned the kiss molten hot until she was crawling onto his lap.

Once she told him about the baby, everything would change. She wanted that one last drop of pure happiness before reality rained down on their passion.

One last time to be with Jon knowing for certain he was with her because he loved her, because he wanted to be, and not out of some sense of responsibility or duty.

Pulling back just enough to speak she said, “Come to my room? I mean Rick’s room.”

Eyes narrowed with desire, he said, “Gladly.”

The realization that she was a guest in her best friend’s home, sleeping in her brother’s bed, started to sink in. “Is this weird? I mean it’s bad to do this here, right? Darci and Chris are—”

“I don’t care.” Jon set Ali on her feet and stood. Grabbing her hand, he pulled her toward the bedroom.

CHAPTER TWENTY-FIVE

Jon was very aware of the hard outline of the ring box in the pocket of his jacket as he took it off and tossed it on Rick's dresser. He was also very aware that it was indeed Rick's bedroom in Darci's house—but not for the same reason as Ali was worried.

He knew Rick would get over them having sex in his bed. Jon's objection was that Ali was staying here at all. He wanted her home, with him, and he was going to get her back one way or another even if it took making a new home for the two of them to do it.

But that was a worry for later. Jon had something more important to do. He brought his hands to her face and leaned down. "Need you."

"I need you too." Ali repeated his words but with

tears in her eyes.

She was upset. Hell, he was pretty upset himself. He'd asked the woman he loved to be his wife and that had sent her running.

Jon was smart enough to learn from his mistakes. He wasn't going to start a conversation about feelings now.

Words had gotten him in trouble last time. Kissing her never had, so that's what he did.

He kissed her until her tears were forgotten and she was clinging to him so tightly there was no way he'd be able to get her clothes or his off. He was fine with that.

After what he'd been through just being here alive and with her was perfect.

Kissing Ali was like waking up from a coma, opening your eyes and seeing the light for the first time.

Sadly, he knew exactly what that felt like from past experience. He really needed to rethink his career path.

That wasn't going to happen now. Not with Ali, warm and needy, pressed against him.

He pushed everything that wasn't her out of his head. No more thinking about Chris and Darci just on the other side of the hall, or that this was Rick's room, or that he had created a hell of a mess of his relationship for a job that hadn't followed the plan it was supposed to.

Instead he concentrated on the warmth of her mouth as he plunged his tongue between her lips. The curves of her hips beneath his hands as he held her close. The softness of the ugly old flannel pajamas she loved so much. The sound of her soft sighs as she melted against him.

He needed to bury himself in this woman and prove to her they belonged together. Tonight. Forever.

Lifting her, he moved the few steps to lay her on the bed. As she watched he began to strip off the clothes that had frustrated him simply because they were a barrier between them.

When he pulled off his shirt and tossed it onto the dresser, he saw Ali's eyes widen. As she focused on the purple bruising on his torso, he said, "Ali, it's just a bruise. It looks worse than it is."

She swallowed hard enough he saw her throat work, before she raised her gaze to his eyes. "Okay."

He wasn't sure he believed that she could accept he was fine. That she would be able to move past the colorful evidence painting his body proving how close he'd come to not being okay.

He made quick work of getting out of his remaining clothes, leaving them where they fell on the floor, and joined Ali on the bed where he could better distract her.

Pushing her top up, he kissed her stomach and across her breast. In case the hard length between them wasn't enough to convince her, he said, "I'm okay. I swear."

She bit her lip and he knew she was worrying in spite of him telling her not to. He could see he had his work cut out for him.

It was going to take more than words to convince her he was fine. Luckily he'd never been afraid of a challenge. Besides, his best plan to distract her wasn't going to be a hardship for him. Not at all.

He sat up on his knees and tugged her bottoms down. Spreading her legs, he went to work intent on knocking all worry from her head.

Things proceeded fast. Too fast. He was done long before he wanted to be, but there was nothing he could do about it. But they had all night . . .

With that in mind he closed his eyes, content with the weight of Ali's head on his chest.

It seemed that one round of energetic sex on top of the prior night's sleeplessness put Jon out for the count. He was unconscious until the annoying sound of a cell phone alarm knocked him out of his slumber.

He rolled over to find Ali sitting on the edge of the mattress. He reached for her and just missed as she stood.

Jon groaned. "Don't get up yet."

She flipped on the lamp and turned to shoot him a look. "This from the man who is up and out by dawn every day?"

Not on days he was interested in morning sex he wasn't. He kept that to himself. "Why are you up so early?"

"It's a work day for some of us." She moved to the open suitcase on the chair and pulled out a pair of underwear and a bra.

He glanced at the bedside clock. "Yeah, but it's still earlier than you usually get up."

"We have an early meeting at work. Listen. Darci's up too. I have to shower quick and get moving." Ali disappeared into Rick's bathroom.

Now that he listened, he could hear the distant sound of running water from the room across the hallway. Unless Chris had felt the need to rise at dawn to shower, Darci was indeed up this early as well.

With a sigh, Jon figured it was useless to stay in bed. He wasn't one for lounging around in the morning anyway, and he certainly wasn't going back to sleep in Rick's bed after Ali and Darci left for work.

As he reached for his underwear on the floor and got dressed, he got hit with the distinct aroma of hot freshly brewed coffee.

That was exactly what he could use—caffeine.

Since he was already an uninvited guest, he might as well go one step further and help himself to some of Rick and Darci's coffee. He grabbed his shoes and jacket and carrying them out to the living area.

Chris glanced at Jon from behind the vase of peonies on the kitchen island. "Well, I have to say it's a relief to see you."

"Really? Why is that?" Jon dropped his belongings on a chair in the living room and moved to the kitchen island.

"Because if that wasn't you I heard Ali getting busy with last night, that would mean she was stepping out on you. Then I would have been in one hell of a tight spot, wouldn't I? Who do I side with?

My boss and friend or my fiancé's best friend? Either way, somebody's gonna end up mad at me. Nice slap in the face that would be, especially since Darci refuses to do anything with me while Ali is in the house." Raising a coffee mug to his lips, Chris cocked a brow and let that information sink in.

Jon cringed. "Sorry."

"That's a'ight."

"I'll apologize to Darci too." He really needed to get Ali back home.

Chris waved away Jon's offer and slid a mug of steaming coffee onto the counter. "Forget about it. Darci was more excited than Ali sounded that you two had made up."

Jon reached for the cup. "Thanks. And I'm not sure we're made up so let's not get ahead of ourselves."

He knew better than to declare *mission accomplished* prematurely. He wasn't going to call this a done deal until Ali was back home and wearing his ring.

"So I guess flowers do work since you stayed the night. Did you also . . . you know?" Chris tapped his ring finger.

"No. Not yet. One step at a time."

"Gotcha. Soften her up in the bedroom first." Chris waggled his eyebrows and grinned.

Jon rolled his eyes. He hated any part of his private life being on display. Chris being privy to the fact he'd bought a ring was one thing, but having Chris and Darci hear him in bed with Ali was just about more than Jon could handle.

The sooner he put that ring on Ali's finger and got this disagreement behind them, the better. But that wasn't going to happen this morning with her rushing off to a meeting.

His cell vibrated twice in quick succession in his pocket. That was the alert for a message from Hasaan. Not the best timing with Chris standing right there and ever vigilant, but Jon needed to check the message.

He pulled the cell out of his pocket, entered the pass code for the app and opened the private message.

It was an address and a time. They wanted him in D.C. today.

It made sense that now he was back they'd want him to debrief. Pass on everything he'd learned. It was the most important part of the mission. The reason he'd gone there.

But right now, it was the last thing he wanted to do because it would take him away from Ali yet again.

Blowing out a breath, he closed the app and shoved the phone back into his pocket. He looked up to find Chris watching him.

Chris cocked one brow. "*The only easy day was yesterday.*"

Jon tipped his head in agreement with the SEAL motto his friend had quoted.

It was etched above the grinder at the BUD/S compound. It's what every wannabe had to keep in mind while the instructors tried to beat them down mentally and physically to weed out those not strong enough to handle the demands.

Chris might joke around a lot but he was smart and he'd been around the black ops block more than a few times. Jon shouldn't be surprised that even if Chris didn't know specifics, he suspected what Jon was currently dealing with.

The only easy day was yesterday.

For better or worse Jon had to put what happened, no matter how bad, behind him and brace for what was to come next, no matter what that might be.

He'd done it before. Every damn day during Hell Week and then for the rest of his career as he realized the shit never ended and he'd just have to get used to it.

Time moved forward. Life went on. Jon only hoped Ali could.

CHAPTER TWENTY-SIX

As if the smirk Ali got from Chris when she came out of the bedroom wasn't enough, she also had to deal with Jon and her uncertainty of how to act around him after last night.

They'd spent most of the night pretending nothing was wrong, but sex didn't miraculously make problems disappear. Though Jon might hope otherwise, she wasn't going to move back in with him just because they'd had sex.

Jon had obviously been injured during this mysterious assignment, proving the issues she had with his job remained.

On top of it all was the secret she kept from him.

The proverbial elephant was still in the room and seemed bigger than ever given that everyone in the house knew about the baby except for Jon.

That was one thing Ali was going to have to deal with eventually, even with as much as she wanted to avoid it.

"Good morning." Visibly more awake then the last time she'd seen him in bed, Jon came to her. He pressed a kiss to her mouth before he handed her a cup of coffee. "I fixed it for you."

"Thanks." She took a sip and found that Jon had indeed fixed her coffee just the way she liked it, with all the cream and sugar she probably shouldn't be having.

She had cut down on her daily intake of caffeine and started mixing half decaf into her morning cup at home, intent on weaning herself off it completely shortly.

But that wasn't going to happen this morning.

Her not taking the coffee he offered would only make him suspicious. When Jon did find out about this baby, it was going to be from her, not because he was freakishly observant and had guessed.

The three stood in silence for what seemed like a long time, though in reality it probably wasn't. Ali continued to concentrate on her coffee and avoided making eye contact. Jon stood close by, watching her, while Chris stayed safely on the other side of the kitchen island and observed them both.

Things couldn't have felt much more awkward, which is why Ali was immensely grateful when Darci emerged from the hallway.

Ali happily set her mug on the counter. "You ready? We should really leave so we're not late for the meeting."

Darci frowned. "Do I have time to get coffee first?"

"Sure, but we should probably take it to go for in the car . . . so we're not late."

Shooting a glance from Ali to Jon to Chris, Darci nodded. "Okay. Chris—"

"Got it, darlin'. One coffee to go." Looking slightly amused, as usual, Chris reached for the top cabinet and got a cup for Darci, and Ali had hope they'd get out of there without further discussion.

She almost made it to the door, but Jon waylaid her by holding her jacket for her to put on.

As Ali slid her arms inside, he said softly near her ear, "Can I see you tonight?"

Was he setting up a booty call in advance? Maybe it wasn't such a bad idea. They could indulge in one more night of hot sex before her big confession complicated everything.

"Um, okay. I guess."

"Good. I'll pick you up here at seven for dinner."

"Dinner?" She turned to frown at him. There went her one last night of simple sex plan.

"Yes, dinner. A dinner date, in fact. I'll make reservations at Georgio's. Do you need me to drop off clothes for you?"

Georgio's was her favorite restaurant. It wasn't cheap and it was too fancy for just any night out. It was the place he took her to once a year for her birthday.

Today was not her birthday.

"Uh, no. I have something I can wear." Some of Darci's jewelry would dress up the black suit and heels Ali had with her.

"Okay. See you later." Jon pressed a kiss to her lips and then handed her the purse that sat on a chair by the door, sending her off for the day.

Meanwhile, Chris and Darci watched every move. Ali needed to get out of here.

"All right. Bye." Head down she marched to the passenger side of Darci's car and was more than grateful to get away, even if it was only to go to work for a staff meeting.

They were barely out of the driveway when Darci glanced sideways at Ali from across the car. "So . . ."

Sighing, Ali begrudgingly asked, "Yes?"

"Did you and Jon talk last night . . . or were you too busy?"

Ali's face burned with embarrassment. She knew they shouldn't have done anything in the house with Darci there.

"We talked a little."

"Really? So what did he say? Did you work things out? Oh my God, did you tell him about the baby? Are you getting married?"

She waited for Darci to get out all of her questions before even attempting an answer. When Darci finally stopped firing off inquiries, Ali said, "Nothing has changed."

As soon as the words were out of her mouth she realized that wasn't completely right. They'd made a tiny bit of progress. Jon had made an effort, from offering to move just to make her feel confortable in their home together, to leaving her socks on when he stripped her.

It sounded silly but he hated when she wore socks in bed. Really, really hated it. So much that she'd had to stop wearing them and suffer with cold feet when she slept.

But last night, he'd left her socks on. That, combined with the fact he'd given her an unprecedented amount of detail about his last assignment, gave her hope.

Actions spoke so much louder than words. Maybe he really was able to change, right down to his ridiculous pet peeves about her socks. Could little things like that really heal a relationship? She didn't know.

"Not to push you or anything, but you do have to tell him about the baby some time, you know.

Ali didn't need Darci to remind her of that. "I know I have to tell him."

"So when are you going to?" Darci pushed the issue.

"I don't know. Soon." Even just talking about it to Darci had Ali feeling sick to her stomach. How in the world was she supposed to tell Jon?

"What about tonight at the restaurant?"

Ali shook her head. "No. Definitely not."

She wasn't going to do this in a public place. Nor did she want to ruin their dinner . . . or dessert, for that matter. She really loved Giorgio's tiramisu.

Darci shot her a glare. "Well, you'd better make it soon. Your boobs alone are going to give you away."

Frowning, Ali pulled the two sides of her blazer

closer together, refusing to admit that her pregnancy boobs were already noticeable even though her baby bump was not.

Jon might be used to things being shot at him, but this was one bombshell she was pretty sure he'd never see coming.

CHAPTER TWENTY-SEVEN

"You look really nice tonight. I like those pants on you."

The fabric of the black slacks clung to her curves nicely. And the high heels put the most tantalizing sway into her every step.

Looking oddly embarrassed by the compliment, Ali met Jon's gaze and then looked away. "Thank you."

So far the meal had progressed mostly in silence broken occasionally by stilted small talk.

Half of the fault belonged to him. He'd spent the day giving reports on anything and everything he'd seen and heard. It had been basically the equivalent of downloading his brain into the hard drive of the organization that had hired him.

Hell, they'd even hooked him up to a polygraph

and had him meet with a psychiatrist to see if he'd been radicalized.

It was protocol for anyone who'd spent time with the enemy in any capacity, but that didn't mean he had to like it. He was exhausted mentally, but grateful they'd finally let him go.

For a bit there he was afraid they were going to keep him overnight, or so late he'd miss dinner. That would have been one more strike against him with Ali—something he was trying to avoid at all costs.

Jon had driven like a bat out of hell and made it in time to pick her up for their date.

He was here. She was here . . . and here they sat, the silence heavy between them.

Finally, Jon said, "It doesn't have to be so hard, you know."

She glanced up from her Pasta Bolognese. "What doesn't?"

He smiled. "Being on a date with me."

"I guess I'm not used to it." She lifted one shoulder.

"What do you mean?"

She rested her fork on the edge of the plate. "Just that we only go out maybe a couple of times a year."

Jon drew his brows down in a frown. "That's not true."

"I don't mean going to Darci's for a barbecue. I mean a real date, just you and me."

He realized she was right. They'd met on the eve of his deployment at a barbecue at Rick and Darci's and had jumped right into bed that night. The circumstances that followed after he returned had them jumping from zero to dating in record time.

They'd skipped right over the usual getting to know you period. Missed all those awkward firsts couples usually went through together. First date. First meeting each other's friends. The decision of when or if to first have sex.

They'd missed a big part of what probably helped couples stay together for the long haul, the building blocks that kept a relationship strong.

In his defense, he hadn't been looking for a girlfriend when he'd met Ali. He didn't know then that one night with her wouldn't be enough. That she would change how he looked at his life.

That she was *the one*.

He'd resisted all that for a long time. Not any more. "You're right. I'm sorry. We'll make more time for just the two of us. Okay?" he asked.

She bit her lip as her eyes glistened with unshed tears but nodded.

These must be happy tears, right?

What the hell did he know? It was becoming very obvious he didn't understand this woman and her odd response to things recently.

All he did know was that if she was fighting tears over his saying they needed to go out to dinner more, he was afraid to see how she was going to react when the tiramisu showed up with the ring in it.

He started to rethink his plan. Shooting a glance toward the maître de he'd slipped the engagement ring to, Jon wondered if he should abort.

Deciding to let it ride for now, Jon looked over at Ali and realized she still only had water in front of her. They'd both been on edge lately. Maybe a drink would help her relax.

"Did you want a glass of wine with your dinner? I can get the waiter—"

"No. Thanks. I don't want any." She paused and then added, "I'm, uh, on a diet."

Jon drew his brows down. "You don't need to be on a diet. You look great."

If she had put on any weight, he couldn't see it. Besides, he loved Ali's curves. She was built like a real woman, not a stick figure.

"Thank you. I'm just trying to eat a little healthier." She dropped her gaze to her dish and let out a short laugh. "But I obviously make exceptions for homemade pasta."

"As you should." It was good to hear her joke. He grinned, but then started to fear for his plan again. What if she skipped dessert in her effort to eat healthy? "And for Giorgio's famous tiramisu too, I hope."

"Yeah, I think that's a must." Her lips tipped up in a smile.

Phew. Crisis averted.

The discussion of food seemed to disperse the tension between them. Ali loosened up a bit and the rest of the meal was almost normal.

Normal, except for the ball of nerves that had settled in the pit of Jon's stomach as he waited for dessert to be served.

Finally, the leftovers had been taken away and boxed up, and the wait was over. After a meaningful glance in his direction, the server placed the tiramisu in front of Ali.

This was it. Showtime.

Ali smiled at the waiter and thanked him, and then picked up her fork.

"You can share with me. I certainly can't eat the whole thing . . . " Her eyes hit on the ring, stuck artfully in a dollop of whipped cream.

Wide-eyed, she raised her gaze to Jon. He cleared his throat and swallowed away the dryness.

"Ali . . ." He noticed she was shaking her head. Not a good sign, but he wasn't going to give up. "Ali, please. Listen. I know you think I rushed into this but I've taken the time to think and there is no question in my mind I want to be with you and only you. Forever—"

"I'm pregnant." Her whispered words took a second to permeate his brain.

Even then he didn't quite understand them. "What?"

"I'm pregnant," she repeated.

Glancing around to make sure they weren't the center of attention, he leaned in closer and whispered, "I thought you were taking birth control."

"I was. It failed."

He drew in a breath as the emotions started to hit. Fear was chief among them. He'd faced ISIS with less trepidation than he felt now at the thought of being a father.

There was now a tiny life he was completely responsible for. He'd have to raise this child without the benefit of any experience or practice or preparation.

A turmoil of emotions assaulted him, blurring the fear as other feelings began to surface. He could have a son to carry on his name. Or maybe it would be a pretty little girl who'd call him Daddy.

There'd be someone to be with Ali, to keep her company, when he was away.

And someone to love him and remember him long after he was gone from this Earth.

With tears in his own eyes, he looked up at her as something clicked in his overwhelmed mind. "Is this why you ran away the other night when I proposed?"

"Yes."

"Why? Don't you want to get married? Especially now."

"I do want to marry you. But I don't want you to marry me just because you have to because of a baby you never asked for or wanted. I'd rather be a single mother than that."

Single mother, his ass. That was not going to happen.

Jon stood and moved around the table. Dropping to his knees in front of her, he grabbed her hands in his. "Who said I don't want this baby?"

"You said at Darci's that the subject of babies wasn't on the table."

He knew that foolish comment was going to come back to haunt him. "I meant I didn't think it was a discussion we needed to have until after we got married but that doesn't mean that I don't want kids. Ali, I want this baby. I want you as my wife. And the ring in your tiramisu proves I wanted to marry you before I knew anything about the baby."

Reaching up he plucked the ring from the top of the dessert. It was a less elegant proposal than he would have liked. He had to lick off the whipped cream, but once it was clean he took her left hand.

"Marry me." He slid the white gold band with the square cut diamond onto her fourth finger.

She let him, which he chose to take as a good sign. Now if she'd just give him an answer. Raising his gaze to hers, he waited.

Tears spilled from her eyes. She was going to have him bawling in the middle of the restaurant too if she didn't stop.

Finally, she ended his agony and, after brushing away the tears, nodded. She didn't actually say the word yes, but that nod was good enough for him. He rose from his knees and pulled her up with him.

Wrapping his arms around her tight, Jon buried his face in her hair.

He would have been happy to just quietly hold her until they both got a hold of their emotions, but thanks to the venue he had chosen they were destined to be interrupted.

As the restaurant exploded with applause from the other diners who'd seen the proposal, the maître de rushed forward with congratulations. A waiter carrying two glasses of champagne followed.

Ali took a glass but shot Jon a worried glance.

He smiled. “One sip won’t hurt.”

As they clinked glasses, his hand shook. He’d be happy to drink hers as well as his own. He needed it.

A wife and a baby.

The initial shock was starting to fade as he settled into the new reality. The more he thought about it, the further the fear receded.

He could do this. They could do this together.

Reeling her in with one arm, he kissed her hard on the mouth, only pulling away to say, “You’re sleeping at home tonight with me.”

They could discuss later where they’d live permanently—where they’d raise their child—but tonight there was no way in hell she was sleeping at Darci’s.

Red-nosed and adorable she nodded. “Okay.”

CHAPTER TWENTY-EIGHT

"Vegas?" Jon suggested later that night.

Ali wrinkled her nose. "I always felt like that was kind of cheesy."

"Okay." Propped on one elbow next to her in their bed, Jon considered other options. "We can have a big church wedding, if you want."

She didn't look any happier with that idea. "That can take so long to plan and schedule. I'm afraid to wait too long. I'm already starting to show a little."

He leaned down and pressed a kiss to her belly. It didn't look all that different to him. "Not really. Well, except for your chest maybe."

She screwed up her mouth unhappily. "Thanks."

"Believe me, I'm not complaining." He decided to change the subject before she cried again. These pregnancy hormones were proving to be a formidable adversary. He moved on to his next idea. "Justice of the Peace?"

Ali lifted one shoulder. "Maybe."

He raised a brow. "You're going to give me a complex here. That's pretty much all of the suggestions I've got to get us hitched. How about this—you and Darci brainstorm. Come up with a plan and I'll go along with it. Just tell me where to be and when."

"Darci has her own wedding to Chris to plan."

"Exactly. That's why she's the perfect choice to help you. She's got experience."

Ali narrowed her gaze at him. Even though he had thought his own suggestion was pretty brilliant, she didn't look happy. "You don't want to be involved?"

This was going to be an interesting seven or so more months. Jon decided to change tactics. He moved so he was lying on top of her.

"Of course, I want to be involved. All I want is for you to be happy." Groaning, he ran his hands down her body. "Well, maybe that's not *all* I want."

She rolled her eyes. "You always want *that* lately."

"Yup." He nipped at her ear and then pulled back. "Is that a problem for you?"

"No." She smiled.

"Good." More than pleased her mood had swung back from the dark side, he decided to take advantage of it.

Slipping one hand beneath her pajama top, he slid over smooth warm skin on his way toward the lush curve of her breast when she sighed, and not in a good way.

He moved his hand back to the safe zone as Ali asked, "What are you going to do when I'm huge?"

He'd already considered that and he couldn't wait.

"Get creative." He ignored that she shook her head at him indulgently as he leaned in to brush a kiss over her throat. "You know you better get over this aversion to being pregnant because we're not having just this one. I want at least two."

"You're already thinking about number two? Can I please get through this pregnancy before we talk about another?"

"Doesn't hurt to talk. Or do other things. You know, to keep in practice." His gaze swept down her body as he worked one-handed to loosen the tie securing her bottoms. "It's not like I can get you pregnant again while you already are, right?"

"Where have you been hiding all this baby lust all these years?"

Jon shrugged. "I guess I was too busy to think much about it."

His own comment reminded him he had to call Zane.

Things at GAPS were going to have to change. They had plenty of men who worked for them and even more who wanted to. Many of them itching for action and willing to go to some of the worst places on the planet.

In light of recent events, Jon was finally ready to let them, and without him being there to supervise.

It was time he admitted that there was no need for him to be everywhere, doing everything.

Realizing that and admitting it, not only to himself but also to Zane, was some serious progress for the workaholic control freak he'd always been.

His partner was going to be shocked by that phone call. And speaking of calls . . .

"Did you tell Darci yet?" Jon asked.

"That we're engaged?"

"Yeah, that and about the baby."

"It's late. I'll call her in the morning and tell her we got engaged, but she already knew about the baby. Chris too."

"Chris knew?" Jon lifted off his fiancé to stare down at her. "Seriously?"

Ali cringed. "Yeah. Sorry. He was there when I told Darci."

Jon scowled. "Son of a bitch. He didn't even drop a hint."

Ali widened her eyes. "Hey, with all the secrets you two keep for work, the least he could do is keep one for me."

"Yeah, I guess." But Jon was still going to give Chris an earful when he saw him. At least now it made sense why Chris was so invested in them making up.

"Darci asked me to be her maid of honor. But that was before this." She gestured to her belly. "I'm going to be a blimp walking down that aisle."

"Maybe they'll wait until after he or she is born."

"I don't know. She was talking about maybe a fall wedding." Ali sighed. "This was pretty bad timing, huh?"

Jon shook his head. "Nope. It's perfect timing."

Ali frowned. "Why do you say that?"

"Because I don't want to wait even another day to get married. Certainly not until fall like Chris and Darci. Thanks to junior in there, you're not going to make me wait." He laid his palm against her belly and grinned, very happy with the turn of events.

EPILOGUE

Silhouetted by the glow of the bright autumn sunlight streaming through the arched church window, Ali was enough to take his breath away.

Jon closed the short distance between them and pressed a kiss to her cheek. “You look beautiful.”

“You have to say that because I’m carrying your child.”

“I said it because it’s true.” Standing close, Jon spread his hands, spanning the breadth of his wife’s stomach.

It seemed to change daily now, expanding as the baby grew. It wouldn’t be long before he met his son or daughter.

The due date wasn’t for another two weeks but Jon had a hunch she wasn’t going to make it that long. He’d had his theory shot down by all the females in their circle of friends since he was just a man and they thought he couldn't know about these things, but he trusted his gut. They'd find out soon enough who was right.

It seemed crazy to think that soon there would be a new little person living in the bedroom-turned-nursery. They'd been waiting for this day for so many months.

In about twenty minutes, he and Ali would be up on the altar, not as bride and groom, but as Matron of Honor and groomsman.

Today was Darci and Chris's day. Jon and Ali had tied the knot with a lot less fanfare months ago in a small quiet ceremony at the Justice of the Peace.

Jon glanced around them. The wedding guests, both out of town relations and local friends, had already begun filling the small church.

This thing was happening not a moment too soon, in his opinion. Between the risk of Brody getting recalled before his brother's wedding and Ali's ever-growing baby, Jon figured they were on borrowed time as it was.

"Is Darci ready?" he asked after checking the time on his watch.

"Yes. The photographer was taking a few shots of her and her mother and father so he said they didn't need me there. I'm happy to not have to smile for the camera right now. I've got the worst indigestion. I don't know what I could have eaten that didn't agree with me." Ali rubbed her stomach.

Jon studied his wife a bit more closely. "Um,

have you been having . . . intestinal issues."

She frowned at him. "Not that I would have brought this up here and now but yes, I did have to run to the bathroom before. Why?"

"Just trying to figure out what you could have eaten."

When she fell asleep at night he read her pregnancy books. Having that much information in his head could be a curse such as now when she'd listed her symptoms.

He wasn't going to worry her just minutes before her best friend's wedding. He'd keep an eye on her. They'd get through the ceremony and then, if necessary, they could call the doctor.

Pulling her as close as he could with her belly between them, Jon wrapped his arms around her, checking his watch behind her back.

Fifteen minutes and counting.

Chris came around the corner, Brody and Rick flanking him.

"There you are. You ready for this?" Chris asked Jon.

"Me?" Jon laughed. "Yeah. Are *you* ready?"

"Never been readier." Chris grinned.

Ali touched Jon's arm. "I'm going to the ladies room and then to check on Darci."

He looked her over again and finally nodded. "Okay. See you at the altar."

She smiled. "Okay."

Jon watched her walk away until she was out of sight.

When he turned back to the group of men, it was

to find Rick pulling a flask partway out of his pocket. "If anyone needs a little liquid courage, let me know."

As much as he could use a swig right about now, Jon had a feeling he'd need all his wits about him.

The preacher came out of the back room and began doing something up on the altar. Brody nudged Chris in the side with his elbow. "Looks like it's almost show time. Last chance to hightail it out of here."

"I'm good, bro. Thanks."

Even as Chris laughed, Rick frowned at Brody. "Hey, that's my sister you're talking about."

"Relax. I'm kidding. Like Chris would ever leave Darci." Brody scoffed. "I'm surprised he let her spend the night alone last night."

Chris didn't need the stress of these two bickering any more than Jon did today, so it was a good distraction when Zane walked in with his girlfriend Missy on his arm.

"Look who's here. Glad you made it." Jon took a step forward and kissed Missy's cheek before shaking Zane's hand.

"I'm glad we made it too. Traffic from D.C. sucked."

"It usually does," Jon agreed as Zane turned to greet Chris, before moving on to shake Rick and Brody's hands.

Missy glanced around the church. "This is quite a crowd."

Brody snorted. "Just our family from Alabama took up the first three pews. There are a lot of

Cassidy cousins."

"And Grandmother, bless her heart, insisted we invite every single one," Chris added.

Rick tipped his chin toward the front of the church. "Looks like the preacher is signaling us."

Looking excited and not at all nervous, Chris rubbed his hands together. "Let's get this show on the road."

Zane indicated the half empty pew in the back of the church. "We're gonna grab a seat. Good luck, man."

"Thanks." Chris accepted the handshake and spun toward the front of the church. "Let's get me married."

Along with Brody and Rick, Jon lined up in front of the altar beside Chris while strains of music filled the church. Cameras and cell phones were raised as the guests took pictures of what must be quite a sight. Four men in pristine Navy dress whites—medals, ribbons and tridents included—as per the bride's request.

As the minutes ticked down, the song changed. A hush fell over the seated crowd.

Brody's girlfriend Ashley appeared at the far end of the aisle wearing a dress the same rose color as Ali's but in a different style. She was followed by Rick's girlfriend Sierra, wearing yet another version of the same color.

Jon caught a glimpse of the twin expressions on Brody and Rick's faces at the sight of their girls and had to wonder how soon it would be before they were all gathered for the next wedding.

Then it was Jon's turn to be enraptured as Ali appeared. Donning a smile for the cameras she walked slowly toward him, until a crease appeared in her brow and she faltered just a bit in her stride. She recovered quickly but he hadn't missed the misstep.

She reached the end of the aisle, shot Jon a glance and then turned, as did the entire congregation when the song changed one more time.

Everyone in the church stood, their eyes on the bride and her father. Everyone except for Jon. His focus was on Ali alone.

He saw her lay one hand on her stomach behind the bouquet she held. He saw her entire body tense as another frown creased her brow. And he saw her hide it all and force a smile when she caught him watching her.

Taking a deep breath, he steadied himself to get through this ceremony without losing his mind, because if his guess was correct his wife was in labor.

Luckily it was a short service. Finally, the vows were said, the rings exchanged and the groom had kissed the bride. Then, thank God, Jon could take Ali's arm as they followed the newlyweds out.

The moment he got his hand on her, he leaned low. "Are you having pains?"

"I'm sure it's nothing. It's probably that Braxton Hicks I read about."

He took that answer as a yes. She was having pain. "We're calling the doctor."

"No, we're going to stand in the receiving line next to Chris and Darci, then we're going to take pictures and then we're going to support them during their first dance."

All of that was going to take hours. The procession stepped outside into the warmth of the sun. He was about to pull her to the side so they could discuss the insanity of her wanting to wait when Ali doubled over.

First dance, be damned. Jon bit back a curse and wrapped an arm around Ali to hold her upright. "We're going to the hospital."

"Okay."

Her agreement threw him off balance. "Okay? You're not going to fight me?"

"No, because I think my water just broke."

Now that the moment was upon him, he was afraid he might collapse right alongside her. Hell of a lot of help he'd be, laid out on the ground as she went into labor.

"What's wrong?" Ashley was next to them in seconds, bending low and trying to see Ali's face.

Somewhere from deep within the chaotic mess his mind had become Jon remembered something. Brody's girlfriend was a nurse.

"Her water broke."

"All right. It's going to be fine. Just breathe, Ali. Slowly." As Ashley became the calming force among them, a crowd formed. Soon it included the bride and groom.

"Oh my God. Are you all right?" Darci ignored the fact she was in white and squatted down with the rest of them on the grass.

Ali let out a short laugh. “Would you hate me very much if I had to leave?”

“What’s wrong?”

“She’s in labor,” Ashley answered Darci’s question.

Chris’s eyes grew wide. “Jesus. You gotta get to the hospital. Do you need an ambulance?”

“I don’t know. Do we?” Jon asked Ashley, the only one who really knew what to do.

“How close are the pains?” Ashley asked Ali.

“I had one before the ceremony started and one just now.”

Ashley turned to Jon. “How far is the hospital?”

“Ten minutes. Five the way I’m gonna drive.”

She smiled. “No need. You should have plenty of time.”

The crowd thickened. Chris dispatched Brody and Rick to wrangle the guests and move them farther away. Former teammates Thom, Grant and Rocky pushed closer offering to help, to carry Ali if needed.

Meanwhile Zane had his cell out offering to get an ambulance, or a chopper if needed.

It was getting overwhelming for Jon, and he was used to chaotic pressure. He could only imagine what Ali was feeling.

But his wife was strong. Ali turned to him. “Help me stand.”

He nodded and helped her up.

She blew out a breath and squeezed Jon’s hand. “I’m okay to get to the truck. Are you sure you can drive?"

A valid question, he supposed, given his panic just a few minutes ago, but he was better now. "Of course, I can drive. I'm not the one having a baby."

She tipped her head and turned toward Darci and Ashley. "You go back to the guests. We're going to the hospital. We'll call you when we have news."

Darci looked a bit shell shocked. "But—"

"I'm good. Really. Don't make me more upset that I ruined your wedding day. You have to do what I say. I'm in labor."

Jon looked to Ashley, hesitant to leave his one connection to a medical professional at a time like this.

She smiled. "It's gonna be fine. Call Brody's phone if you need to. I'll stay right there next to him."

"Thank you." Jon turned his dazed gaze from Ashley to Chris and Darci. "I'm so sorry. We have to go. We'll call as soon—"

"Jon. Go." Chris grabbed Jon's shoulder and physically turned him toward the parking lot.

He forced himself to walk at Ali's pace, even though he would have been happier picking her up and sprinting for the vehicle.

When they finally reached the truck and she had to struggle to get into the high cab, he cursed himself for not taking her car. It would have been so much more comfortable for her.

Too late for regrets.

After running around the front end, he climbed into the driver's seat, shaking as he shoved the key into the ignition. He glanced across at Ali. If anything happened to this woman he didn't know what he'd do.

He cut off that thought and asked, "You okay?"

"Yes." She smiled. "Are *you* okay?"

He dropped his gaze to her belly and then brought it back up to the face of the woman he would love until the day he died. "No, but I will be."

~ * ~

Birth Announcement

Jon and Alison Rudnick of Virginia Beach, Virginia, announce the birth of their son, James Matthew Rudnick, born October 22, 2016.

~ * ~

Hot SEALs

Night with a SEAL
Saved by a SEAL
SEALed at Midnight
Kissed by a SEAL
Protected by a SEAL
Loved by a SEAL
Tempted by a SEAL
Wed to a SEAL
Romanced by a SEAL
Rescued by a Hot SEAL

For more titles by Cat visit CatJohnson.net

ABOUT THE AUTHOR

Cat Johnson is a top 10 *New York Times* bestseller and the author of the *USA Today* bestselling Hot SEALs series. She writes contemporary romance featuring sexy alpha heroes and is known for her unique marketing. She has sponsored pro bull riders, owns a collection of camouflage and western wear for book signings, and has used bologna to promote romance novels. A fair number of her book consultants wear combat or cowboy boots for a living.

Never miss a new release or a sale again. Join Cat's inner circle at catjohnson.net/news.

Made in the USA
Lexington, KY
22 May 2017